The Not So Stories

By

Rod Griffiths

Black Pear Press

The Not So Stories

Rod Griffiths

ISBN 978-0-9565263-7-3

Published by Black Pear Press
www.blackpear.net

Cover art work Lois Parker

Dedicated to Lois, and all the other people in Worcestershire and elsewhere, particularly those at "42" and "Speakeasy" who have listened to many of these stories and laughed in the right places.

Other works by Rod Griffiths

Side Effect – Like a Rag Doll Falling
ISBN 978-0-9565263-0-4

Aimless Fear
ISBN 978-9565236-2-8

Individual short stories in
Short Stories from Black Pear
ISBN 978-0-9927755-0-6

Flashes of Fiction
ISBN 978-0-9927755-1-3

You Can't be Serious
ISBN 978-0-9565263-9-7

The Unbroken Circle
ISBN978-1-906198-04-6

Index

Introduction

I have always admired Kipling's Just So Stories. Kipling, was expansive in his style and enjoyed playing with words. For example, we are told that the Whale *"ate the Starfish and the Garfish, and the Crab and the Dab, and the Plaice and the Dace, and the Skate and his mate, and the Mackereel and the Pickereel and the really Twirly-Whirly Eel."* It is charming and quirky but hardly punchy. My stories are shorter. They have been developed in performances at story-telling gigs where time and word counts are limited. I aim to be at least mildly funny because in live performances laughter works so much better than tears.

Some of the charm of Kipling's stories is in his use of simple questions: *How did the Tiger get his stripes*? *How did the camel get his hump?* Kipling did not exhaust all such questions, so I thought it might be fun to explore a few more, like "Why do swallows sit on phone wires?" and "Why pigs don't fly". I have tried to imagine explanations that are vaguely plausible, though clearly impossible. None of these stories are true, or at least not completely true, hence they are Not So Stories.

I should digress here to mention my grandmother because she probably told me more stories than anyone else. Grandma Evans read a great deal and watched TV much of the time. She also knitted. She clearly had a very advanced brain because somehow she could read a book, knit and watch TV at the same time. These activities became

1

one continuum in her mind, so that when she knitted supposedly identical sweaters for me and my two brothers, we actually had no difficulty telling them apart because each had been constructed at a different point in the plot, and hence, to a different pattern. Sometimes her stories were hard to follow, possibly because a knitting pattern became woven into the narrative. I suspect that my love of obscure twists comes from her.

In another departure from Kipling, I have to say that these are not children's stories, though they are not about what is commonly called adult material; they are simply a little more complicated or in some cases require some background knowledge before the reader is likely to get the point. In some cases the logic may appear a little twisted or even quirky. Put that down to Grandma.

There are other stories, some of which have a common theme; "String Theory" three stories, "Zombies" four stories and "Gordis Thriff" five Stories. A little more background to these is included at the start of each of those sections. Two of the String Theory stories also fit the "Why Do..." format, but are included in the String Theory section.

The largest group of stories are an eclectic mixture whose inspiration comes from a number of sources. Often the themes or titles were invented by a writing group, the largest number coming from Worcester Writers' Circle, who publish their titles on their web site each year, so anyone can play, even if you don't come to the group.

Why Pigs Don't Fly

Have you noticed how when we say, "If pigs could fly," it's often with a tinge of regret. Why would that be? Maybe they did fly once, and we have some sort of race memory of a more interesting past.

Pigs don't fly, we all know that, but why don't they? Pigs are clever; it is no accident that George Orwell had them running Animal Farm. You might think that was because he was trying to make a point about plutocratic bosses with their snouts in the trough. That may well be, but it is also true that psychologists have done experiments showing that pigs are clever. Smarter than dogs for instance. So why don't they fly?

Pigs have a streamlined shape; look at them twice and it's obvious that they resemble torpedoes. That pointed nose, apart from the flat bit at the end, could have been taken from a Concorde, well, a short fat Concorde anyway. Pigs have short legs, so if they bridged across the gap to their body with folds of skin, like flying squirrels do, then the pigs would have short stubby wings. That works, but only at high speed, and that's where the problems arise.

Pigs make plenty of gas; you only have to spend some time near a pig farm and that is obvious. Igniting the gas is not a problem: a couple of bits of steel on the back legs and the pig can easily produce a spark, so jet propulsion is definitely a possibility. The actual flame must be a couple of inches behind the pig, and that requires some muscular coordination. Thus pigs soon learn that failure to emit the gas fast enough burns their arse off. This only has to happen once to establish enough motivation to ensure that the pig goes really fast every time.

Take off and landing is another issue. High-speed flight needs a long runway and pigs are often kept in small fields, so getting up enough speed to clear the fence is very tricky, and landing is even harder. That's the problem with having a torpedo-like shape, darn difficult to slow down unless you crash into something, in which case, with all that burning gas, the resemblance to a torpedo becomes even more striking.

All that can be overcome, but the big problem is keeping the supply of gas going. The pig can eat fast, you only have to watch them at the trough to know that, but eating fast enough to power up the jet and eating enough for a long trip is hard. The ones that can do it tend to grow so fat while they are practising that they never get off the ground. They take a bit of a run at it, click their heels to make a spark and turn themselves into stationary flame throwers that do no end of damage.

Research has been done to cut down on the fuel load by eating a concentrated protein mixture that can produce massive amounts of methane very quickly. It would do the job, there's no doubt about that, but it tastes terrible, and the pigs won't touch the stuff.

That's it really, the fundamental reason pigs don't fly is because they're too smart—it's too much bother, just not worth the hassle, especially when, with the right persuasion, farmers will give you food all the time and plenty of muck to play in.

Why Swallows Sit on Phone Wires?

You may have noticed lines of swallows sitting on phone wires. If you get close, you will hear that they often sing while they sit there. It is easy to jump to the conclusion that they are simply having a rest, having flown all the way from Africa, but that's not why they are there.

If you watch swallows all through the summer, you will see that one of the first things the grown ups do with their babies, very soon after they leave the nest, is to teach them to sit on the wires. If they are good and don't fall off, then they get fed.

Phone wires are a recent creation: Alexander Graham Bell only invented the telephone in 1876, a while ago, I agree, but swallows have been visiting every summer since long before that.

Back in the years when men first made villages, every house had eaves and roofs made of thatch. Every year swallows came from Africa, but back in those days, Africa was not very far away. Continents drift around, you know, floating like plates on the liquid rocks at the nearer to the middle of the earth. Of course, that's another story for another day.

Back in those days, swallows were lazy birds, and found it easy to rest in the nice warm thatch that could be found in every village. Life was pleasant for those swallows back then, because the thatch was a great place for insects to live and breed. The swallows hardly had to fly at all, just roll out of bed and whiz around the house once or twice, and they could find all the food that they wanted.

As the continents drifted apart Africa got further away, and the swallows had to learn to fly faster and farther to come to England in the summer. They were tired when they arrived, but as the years went by more and more people were born and made more and more houses so there were always plenty of places to stay. You can imagine how pleased the little birds were when they crossed the English Channel each year and, in no time, they would spot a nice house for the summer. If some other swallow family got there before them, there was no problem. They just flew along the road or maybe to the next village, and there would be a roof ready for them. Year by year, tiles and bricks replaced the thatch, but there were still barns and cowsheds, and other places to stay.

Back in those days, it has to be said that people weren't very tidy; they used to throw rubbish out of windows, and we all know where there's rubbish there are insects flying around just above it. The swallows had to learn to swoop close to the ground to get their food, but that was no problem, they'd spent time developing wings to fly to Africa, so a few aerobatics while on summer holidays was no more than idle entertainment.

As time went by, people started living in big blocks of flats and solid concrete buildings with no thatch and no eaves, and it got harder for the poor swallows to find places to stay. They had to fly further and search more. Food got harder to find as well, because the people became tidier and kept their rubbish in bins and the only place where you could find a lot of it was great big rubbish tips. That might have been all right but the seagulls came and lived there all the year round and they were much bigger than the swallows. The swallows had to fly even further and even faster to find their food.

Then the people started converting barns into houses and knocking down old buildings and building new ones. They made great big roads and car parks, all covered in concrete and tarmac, so the swallows could only live out in the country. Finding a house for the summer became even harder.

Life was hard for the swallows; Africa was a long way away by now, and even though they had learned to fly very fast, with their swept-back wings and streamlined tails, they might have found nowhere to stay. The last thing you want to do, if you've just flown all the way from Africa, is to be hunting around all over the place for the right kind of roof.

Right about then the swallows got lucky because the humans invented the telephone. All over the country, they strung wires on poles and the swallows soon found that if they perched on the wires they could feel the messages with their feet.

Swallows are clever little birds; after all they manage to fly to Africa and back every year without getting lost and not many people can do that. Once they had learned about reading the wires, it didn't take long before they could make messages themselves. That was just what they needed to secure a house for the summer. They could sit on a wire in South Africa and phone England to make sure of a place to stay. When they got across the channel, they'd just have a sit on a wire for ten minutes to call and check that the booking was OK, and let everyone know when they would be arriving.

Sitting on a wire and not falling off has become a very important skill for baby swallows to learn; after all, no one wants to be homeless. So that's why the very first thing the swallows teach their babies is how to fly around and get back into the nest; perhaps you've seen them doing it. Right after that, they are taught to sit on wires and practise singing. They are very unsteady at first, but they practise every day.

They don't just sit; their parents feed them, they learn to preen their wings, and they begin to sing. Why do they spend so much time on the wires? I imagine that the swallow booking service is no better than BT; they probably keep you on hold for ages, so they have to learn how to pass the time.

You may not believe this, but try listening to a swallow's song. If you have ever dialled the number of a fax machine by mistake, you'll know that it sounds just like a swallow singing.

Why There Are No Magic Carpets?

Stories used to be full of magic carpets, well that's the way my childhood memory tells it. It is of course possible that my recollection is faulty, or maybe those who told me stories when I was young had a particular love of magic carpets. That could be it. My dad was a pilot and I know it was the flying that he loved and not all that business with engines, petrol, airports and such. Flying on something that you could just step onto would have been attractive.

There is a rational explanation, from a literary point of view. Back in those days there was no obvious mechanism available to the storyteller that allowed rapid transport between different places. If you had to use camels or wagon trains, then there are a whole lot of additional issues, like stopping for food, repairing wagon wheels, avoiding Indians and surviving dodgy hotels that have to be included in the story to give it any sort of credibility. Use a magic carpet, on the other hand, and your story can take flight.

If you believe that premise, then magic carpets were bound to disappear once Star Trek had invented beaming up. More prosaically you can blame trains, planes or flying saucers; all of them can beat the hell out of a magic carpet

Believe all that if you like, but that's not it at all.

The real answer lies in the culture and ethnography of carpets.

Carpets in the olden days took time to make. Thread or yarn had to be made and dyed to get the colours. It had to be cut to lengths, mounted on a loom and woven into patterns. All this took time, and it needed a place to do it. It needed care and skill and contemplation, and with that comes a sense of culture and pride. It needed inspiration as well, and that doesn't happen every day. Inevitably piles of yarn stood around, red in one corner, blue in another, alongside half made carpets and those ready to sell.

All that passage of hours and days meant that the carpets had time to talk. Leaning against each other in the crowded dusty sheds, what else was there to do? There was time for colours and memories to bleed into each other and pass on the magic. That's how flying carpets were born, carpets filled with inspiration and knowledge, ready to fly above the world to the places buried deep in their collective memories.

In a modern factory the yarn arrives on drums, it's cut and woven in hours not months and it's out of the warehouse and into shops in no time. Cheaper foam-backed carpets are even worse, the yarn is chopped into lengths so short they can remember nothing and they are glued together with chemicals that make you dizzy. The whole process is vertically integrated and run on just-in-time delivery. There is no time to stand and talk, and there is no magic any more.

Why NASA Didn't Invent the Kindle?

You would think a Kindle would have been immensely valuable in an environment where both space and weight are restricted. It would probably have helped sell them as well, and provided an answer of sorts to all those people who keep banging on about traditional books being so wonderful (which they are). The notion that the space age required something different surely would have had some traction.

9

There are also modern arguments in favour of books, like carbon capture for instance. If the entire population of the world had ten extra books each, would it capture enough carbon to make up for all that rocket fuel?

The space programme is sometimes justified by the stimulus it gives to invention. The biro that will write on the ceiling is often cited as an example. I've no doubt that tall people can understand that, but I would have thought they could do better, which brings me back to the Kindle.

Anyone who is an avid book reader is bound to wonder what the astronauts did with their time while they were whizzing round and round the world. It's like sitting in a very small apartment for a long time; surely they missed having books.

I'm sure they didn't take a pile of books with them, because the weight would be too much, though we do know from watching the Apollo 13 movie that at least one astronaut sneaked a small tape recorder on board. If they did take books, someone would have been advertising those books by now as the best book to take into space with you.

I caught a radio programme the other day that explained it all. They spent their free time looking out of the window. The programme was comparing the Challenger ocean exploration voyage a hundred odd years ago with the space exploration by the shuttle. The Victorian pioneers apparently did read books when they were pottering along in quiet seas, but the spacemen looked out of the window.

I don't want to imply that this means that the space men were somehow not up to the mental task of reading, because we know that they are all both physically and intellectually top performers. What it does tell us is something of just how captivating and completely original the view from a spaceship must be. An experience so novel that it has to be watched whenever possible.

Another snippet of the programme explained that although the physical environment of the space station is restricted. (I'm struggling here not to say there is no space in a space station). You can, however, make the most of it because weightlessness means that the ceiling is as good as the floor or walls to store things, hence wanting a biro that will write on the ceiling. What they didn't do was store things near portholes because the crew wanted to spend their free time sitting there and looking out.

All this is hearsay from a radio programme, so it may not be true, but it suggests that if the spaceship had no windows we might have had the Kindle years ago.

Why Pigeons Coo

Pigeons have the most annoying song. Coo, Coo or sometimes coocoocoo pause coocoo, as the one on our chimney used to say. Many other birds can manage something more interesting, yet pigeons are said to be intelligent. Apparently, in experiments, they could spot a painting by Picasso, even one that they hadn't seen before, just by recognising the style.

Not only that but they are able to navigate vast distances because they have some sort of satnav built into their brain, and they know how to work it, which is more than can be said for some humans. They are clumsy fliers, taking off from trees with much bashing of wings into branches and general thrashing about. Even when they are airborne they rarely keep up the wing beats for more than a few flaps, going forward in great swoops with periods of gliding often longer than the active flight. It is as though their minds were on something else and they only remember now and then that they are supposed to be flying.

They spend a lot of time on the ground, frequently following members of the opposite sex. In cities where there is an abundance of food, mostly provided by humans, they can apparently breed all year round, and do so, potentially producing six broods a year.

Of course, it's not all sex and art, they have been known for some great feats of heroism, delivering messages from battlefields, stricken aircraft and spies, sometimes in the face of serious danger. The Dickin medal is awarded for animal heroism, and pigeons are the only birds that have ever won it, along with many dogs, a few horses and one cat (it got rid of rats on a battleship).

It is of course possible that they were taught to make their idiotic cooing noises as a cover in case of capture. Many birds have different dialects, depending on where they live, and perhaps it was thought that skilled ornithological interrogators would be able to extract some useful information if the birds were allowed to say whatever they felt like. Indoctrinating them to stick to coo coo could be a cunning ploy to fool the enemy. On the other hand a message tied around your leg is a bit of a give away, so while this is an attractive explanation to anyone with a strong bent towards conspiracy theory, it doesn't really wash.

Try to research why pigeons coo and more than likely you'll come up with references to pigeon English rather than the birds. This may be simply a quirk of Google's algorithm or it may have a deeper significance—back to conspiracies again. The most likely explanation goes back to their intelligence work and the

answer is probably well hidden somewhere inside GCH
COO.

Why the Earth is Round

Long, long ago when the earth was flat, and
dinosaurs were very, very big, Tyrannosaurus Rex, a very
big dinosaur, decided to eat meat. The vegetarian
dinosaurs thought it would be a good idea to get as far
away as possible.

What they didn't know was that if a great big
heavy dinosaur goes to the very edge of a flat planet, then
the edge is bound to bend a bit. Before long the earth
wasn't flat at all, it was bent at the edges, like an upside
down saucer. You can imagine what happened, most of
the water ran off, all that was left were some very deep
puddles and they soon got very muddy.

Everyone ran to the edge of the world to see
where the water had gone, and that made it bend more
and more, until the edges came to meet each other and it
ended up round. By then all the animals were standing
where the edges met, which made the earth much heavier
on that side, so it began to fall down through space.

That was lucky, because it caught up with the
water.

The animals didn't want to drown, so they ran for
their lives, which made the earth begin to spin. Millions
of years later Isaac Newton proved that this was bound
to happen if they all ran the same way. It was lucky they
did, because it spread the water all round the world and
gave us days and nights.

We can thank the dinosaurs for giving us a round earth that is spinning though space. It didn't do them much good though, the big heavy ones couldn't run fast enough, so they drowned and became fossils.

How Deep is the Ocean?

That's a trick question.

Why?

Because there is more than one ocean, if you don't say which one, then no one could answer.

How deep is the biggest ocean?

That's better but it still won't do.

Why?

Because you didn't say what you mean by biggest. Do you mean the widest? Or the deepest? Or the one with the biggest volume of water? Or the one with the longest name? There are many ways of being the biggest.

The deepest. How deep is the deepest ocean?

That's not really a fair question either.

Why?

Because to answer it I'd have to know how deep all the oceans were, in order to know which one was deepest, so really you are asking five questions.

Why?

Because most people think there are five oceans.

When you look at a globe it looks like one ocean.

Yes but no one knew that when they got their names.

What are their names?

Atlantic, Pacific, Indian, Arctic and Antarctic, but now they call that one the Southern Ocean.

Which is the biggest?

The Pacific.

And which is the deepest.

The Mariana Trench in the Pacific, it's 35800 feet deep. If you stood the highest mountain in it, all of it would still be underwater.

Why do you answer all my questions?

Because I'm your dad.

Why?

Ask your mother.

An Introduction to String Theory

String Theory is a current theory prominent in physics and I suspect that outside that field no one else has any idea what it means. I will admit to trying to read about it, and very entertaining it is too. I have never before read material where I would not be able to explain what a single sentence meant. It appears that there are many others who have the same problem; even the experts have difficulty. I found one brilliant quote *"It is therefore simultaneously the best time for someone to read a book on the topic and the worst time for someone to write one."* (from Introduction to String Field Theory. Advanced Series in Mathematical Physics Vol. 8 Warren Siegel).

I think that is probably the most elegant way I have seen someone write that no one fully understands the subject.

In the circumstances it seemed OK to come up with a String Theory of my own. I could have called this section an alternative string theory, but as no one seems to really know what the physics one is, then mine may be true after all.

String Theory

Windsor Knott was a daydreamer. He would muse for hours over such simple questions as why do shoelaces always come untied, whereas string left to its own devices always tangles? Is this part of some fundamental law of the universe, some deep symmetry, equal amounts of twist and untwist, like matter and antimatter?

If all the unattended string in the world was left tidy, rolled onto reels, or kept from tangling in some devious way, would all the shoelaces stay tied? Shoe laces are string, but their natural state is to be tied in knots, at least during the day. At night they are untied, but most people are asleep then, so the properties of any other string in the neighbourhood matters little, unless you are camping of course. These issues taxed the mind of Windsor Knott.

These thoughts kept him awake at night. Fortunately even his speculations usually achieved some balance. If a camper untied all his shoelaces before getting into his sleeping bag, then it should make the knots in the guy ropes stay tight. What a relief he thought, and fell asleep. On a bad night it crossed his mind that if a camper wore slip-on shoes, this could be dangerous, the tent might collapse in the night. Dreamless anxiety would overcome him until balance was re-established by the thought that campers often put up washing lines, long stretches of perfectly straight string.

It was only a matter of time before his inventive mind began to speculate that perhaps these properties of string could be exploited. What if an army of people, or possibly small robots constructed for the purpose, were to go around deliberately tying spare string in more and more knots? The implication seemed clear; shoelaces would come undone with every increasing frequency, simply in order to maintain the balance. The great unknown was the range that the effect might operate over. Did it diminish on an inverse square, like many other field effects, or was it linear?

Several weeks of feverish research were required to produce and then mass produce miniature string tangling automated robots, STARs for short. He fitted the back of his van with an array of STARs in order to conduct his first experiments. He met the 5.27 from Waterloo to Richmond. He parked outside the station and set the robots to work on a pile of string in the back of his van, just as the train arrived. Chaos ensued as 400 city gents, in pinstripe suits and shiny black shoes, exhausted after a hard day making money, had to contend with stepping on each others loose shoelaces as they rushed home. Fortunately, there were no fatalities, and only two divorces; a figure a mere 3% above the seasonal average. Alcohol consumption, however, rose by 19%.

Mr Knott then miniaturised his robots in order to fit hundreds in a suitcase. They could spin tiny threads into multiple knots at amazing speed. With vast numbers of these miniature STARs in one place, he could create a local concentration of tangled string that would generate a massive pressure to make any knot in the vicinity untie itself. Installing himself in a strategic position close to tube stations frequented by the staff of major stockbrokers, he made a small fortune by short-selling stocks on the days his robots caused shoelace chaos.

With this capital he started his next business. His studies of string theory suggested that if the natural tendency of string to tangle were resisted then energy must be expended. He reasoned that this energy has to come from somewhere, before it disappears into the string. If all other possible sources are removed, then the only place the energy can come from is the surrounding environment and hence there must be a cooling effect. Knott had discovered a new method of refrigeration and using his gains from his adventures in the stock market he was able to build a massive refrigeration and air-conditioning business.

A side effect of his brand of domestic refrigerators was of course that the owners never suffered an undone shoelace at home; an added source of contentment, which may have subliminally led them to recommend his products to their friends and further increase sales. Similarly his industrial models ensured the same effect in businesses that bought them, thus producing a slight gain in productivity, staff contentment and industrial relations.

Knott also embarked on a more ambitious project to create a new form of domestic air conditioning. His idea was quite simple: if the cavity walls of houses could be filled with string that could be straightened or tangled by his robots, depending on the outside temperature, then a very efficient form of air conditioning could be created. Knott encountered two problems. The first was mice, which had a tendency to chew off small bits of string and use them to make nests. The second problem was spiders. Spider's webs are very efficient combinations of curved and straight string. (See 'Why Spiders Make Webs' for more details). Knott appreciated the genius of spiders but they made his equations more complicated, so they had to go. He equipped his robots with small laser cannons that could kill a spider two feet away. Mice were a problem in two ways, not only did they chew up the string but their straight tails also caused problems. Fortunately they learned to keep away from the robots. (See also 'Why Mice Have Straight Tails').

The spiders on the other hand have been done an injustice. They responded to string theory through an evolutionary process. (See 'Why Spiders Make Webs'). The spider's web combines just the right amount of curve and straightness to maintain equilibrium. The evolution of the various possible patterns was a matter of survival for the arachnids, because any excess tendency to tangle rapidly led to fatal complications in a species with eight legs. Suspending their webs from straight strings added another small influence for which they have never been thanked; helping to keep shoelaces tied, at least until the owner ventured outdoors.

The whole house air conditioning business was largely thwarted by the cavity foam industry, but despite this Knott made enough money from his fridges to be able to turn his attention to his real love; space travel. How could the energies involved in string theory be used to power spaceships? he mused, and hit upon the solution by accident.

When setting up his suitcase full of robots he always ensured that only a proportion were in action at once, in order to keep some spare capacity in reserve, and avoid the risk of over-heating.

As he made more money from the cooling business he worried less, until one hot evening, feeling rather mellow and sipping a glass of wine that was a little too warm, he thought it might be amusing to see if he could produce a solid block of ice. Stuffing an old backpack full of spare robots, he soaked the outside with a measured quantity of water and then set his remote control on one hundred per cent straightening from all the robots in the pack.

To his considerable surprise, the bag froze completely solid and seemed to squash and distort for a split second into a sort of flattened pyramid, before shooting across the room, demolishing the wall, and scattering a mixture of brick rubble and ice fully a hundred yards down the garden.

Being a methodical man, it took him the best part of a day to chart the final resting point of all the fragments, weigh them, add in the mass of the added liquid, and calculate the energy involved in the explosion.

Months of theoretical work on string theory followed. Why had the backpack moved? A simple explanation puts it like this. When all the strings are untangled and neat, an entity is created which is so alien that the surrounding universe rejects it, and therefore applies a crushing force. Inevitably, the object behaves like an orange pip squeezed from all sides, and flies off in the line of least resistance. Fortunately, Knott had selected a package that was narrower at one end.

Had he, for instance, believed in flying saucers, which lack any pointy aspect, a catastrophe would have ensued. Such a shape would be simply crushed out of existence, releasing energy on the well know $e=mc^2$ formula and causing a detonation of several megatons, preventing any further calculation.

He launched his first rocket from the roof of a nearby tower block. He filled the rocket with miniature robots and built in a radio control in order to be able to retreat a safe distance before firing He could also shut off the power by telling the robots to change string mode. By cunningly arranging the machines in concentric circles inside the shell, he hoped to achieve some steering effect by connecting the arrays of robots to a joystick on his radio remote control.

He hit full power to launch and was astonished when the rocket simply disappeared, the only evidence of flight being a hole punched in the clouds high above. He rapidly sent instruction to turn around and return to earth, but as radio waves only travel at the speed of light and his creation had travelled six light years before it stopped, he put the experiment down as a failure. Later, adopting the more standard jargon of scientific discovery, he called it a modified success; it did take off, after all. He returned to the drawing board, and fortunately was not in the area six years later when the tower block was demolished by what was assumed to be a meteor strike.

Once the theory was sorted out, manned space flight over interstellar distances became possible. There were of course a few minor hiccoughs on the way. The orange pip, or wet soap squeezing, method of propulsion simply launches the craft towards the nearest region of space where there is the least matter available to be offended by too much straight string.

This is not a destination on any space tourist's wish list. It's peaceful there, but has little else to recommend it. Such places are hard to get back from, because no amount of telling the robots to change their string configuration produces any great thrust from the two or three atoms available in deep space. They are as lost and pissed off with their plight as the poor thankless robots sitting in the spacecraft. Fortunately, he soon discovered that switching to neutral, and freewheeling before it actually stops, is enough to get the rocket to a more crowded piece of space where propulsion can be achieved.

As he prepared for manned flight, Knott thought the prodigious acceleration might flatten any astronaut against the wall. Experiments with squashy dolls and other similar dummies, viewed by on-board web cam, revealed a more comfortable scenario. The creation of a small sub-universe, under the influence of an excess of straight string, meant that the complete entity moved as a whole when squeezed, and retained its inner relationships, thus ensuring the safety of the pilot.

The first manned flight did unfortunately end in tragedy. The pilot became obsessed with the notion that such a momentous event required some formality and ceremony. Accordingly, he dressed rather formally with suit and tie under his space suit, sporting a Windsor knot in homage to the inventor. The web cam footage showed the usual rapid take-off followed by the pilot going red in the face shortly before slamming into Mars. Initially, Knott thought that the phenomenal acceleration had resulted in a red shift in the pictures coming back from the web cam, in much the same way that galaxies moving away from the earth at near light speed appear red to astronomers. Further study revealed the tragic truth. The tie, striving to correct the excess of straight string, had tied itself more and more firmly around the pilot's neck, and strangled him before he could touch the controls to slow down and land.

Why Spiders Make Webs

Spiders evolved at least 300 million years ago, which is about 100 million years before birds and mammals. Spiders have eight legs, we all know that, but some of their ancestors had ten, the front two were used to handle food, leaving eight to get around with. Over the course of the next couple of hundred million years, the creator, or evolution, whichever you prefer, realised that four or even only two legs were quite adequate for getting around, but spiders were stuck with eight.

As we know, string theory suggests that an excess of straight string will lead to tangles. Avoiding getting your legs tied in knots was a crucial problem that spiders had to overcome if they were ever going to be able to move fast enough to avoid cleaners wielding feather dusters. Of course at the time spiders had no way of knowing that they had just under 300 million years to get it right; for all they knew some human might come trotting into view at any moment. The poor things had only just seen off the dinosaurs, so they probably though there was no time to lose.

Initially, they settled for having short legs, so short that they were impossible to tangle. This is not a bad solution: centipedes and woodlice went down that road. It works and, if you can get your nervous system wired up right, you can even go quite fast, but you are so close to the ground that it is hard to see where you are going. Is it any surprise that these creatures tend to live in dark places or even underground? The fact is that it is all the same to them. If you are that close to the ground, even something like a toenail clipping is a major obstacle. You can climb over it OK but you have no idea what might be on the other side—it could be the creature that is busily cutting its toenails.

Spiders were more ambitious, they wanted longer legs so they could see over all that rubbish but eight long legs were bound to get tied in knots. The solution was the spider's web. This is a brilliant innovation. It uses the very properties of string that cause the problem with longer legs. All the spider had to do was optimise the right amount of curves and joined up string with a balancing amount of straight string, minus a factor for leg length. The maths is a little complicated but maths skills go with the territory if you have eight legs to manage.

The really cunning part is that the process of making the web works a bit like an analogue computer; the leg length of the spider making the web determines the dimensions of the web and the way that it is knotted together. Every spider's web is custom built to fit the spider that made it and optimised so that there is no impediment to being able to run like hell with perfectly aligned legs when the feather duster come along.

Why Mice Have Straight Tails

Three blind mice. Three blind mice.
See how they run. See how they run.
They all ran after the farmer's wife,
Who cut off their tails with a carving knife,
Did you ever see such a sight in your life,
As three blind mice?

Mice have straight tails; always straight and never curly, and such is the nature of evolution that it must have something to do with survival. Either a straight tail gets you more food or it helps you get away, if you're a mouse that is. It doesn't take much to realise that it has nothing to do with escape. Just think about the farmer's wife with her carving knife. Swinging a big implement like that at a small moving target is tricky; make the target three times as long and you can see how she managed to cut off their tails. So, if it's not survival it must be food.

What do mice eat? Cheese. Every one knows that. But what about before cheese was invented? Cheese is complicated; it needs domesticated cows and farmers, as well as a place to keep the stuff while it matures. The mice must have lived on something else, back when men were learning how to tame cows, build barns, and make buckets and, of course, carving knives.

Mice eat spiders; in fact, they'll eat almost anything, though they can be quite choosy. We had a squad of them who invaded our house when we were away one Christmas. They got into some packets of biscuits and somewhat surprisingly ate all the expensive ones. Unfortunately, their taste in baked goods says little about long-term survival and evolution. Biscuits, like cheese, are recent inventions, so we are back to the spiders, centipedes, and woodlice that mice had to live on before they developed expensive tastes.

What do all those creatures have in common? Lots of legs and a need for coordination of said legs in order to get around. Anything long and thin, like spiders' legs, can be classed as string, for theoretical purposes, and is therefore governed by the need for equilibrium across all the forms that string can take. String and string-like objects have a natural tendency to tie themselves in knots or if already tied, to come undone. If there is too much untied string around, then more knots will appear and vice versa, always tending to produce an equilibrium.

This is tricky territory for spiders and centipedes. The latter get around the problem by having very short legs, everyone knows that you can't tie a knot if the string is too short. Spiders have gone to a lot more trouble, weaving complicated patterns in their webs to ensure just the right balance and allow themselves to dash about without their legs becoming tangled. (See "Why Spiders Make Webs").

Along comes a mouse with a long straight tail and the whole thing is thrown into confusion. Spiders were forced to learn how to walk on the ceiling.

That's where the evolution stayed until farmer's wives came along. Not only did they have carving knives but they also invented mousetraps. Having your tail cut off with a carving knife does cramp a mouse's style somewhat. It makes it harder to catch spiders for sure, but along with the knives comes also cheese—win some lose some.

The mice have some tricks of their own. Their straight tails create a field around themselves in which any available knot or tangle will grow tighter. This explains all those Victorian postcards of corseted ladies standing on chairs when they see a mouse. That is, surprisingly, a sensible response, as distance from the mouse reduces the influence of the tail and hence may loosen the corset; in fact, the higher the stool the woman jumps on, the better. The maximum leap possible in a corset that is already becoming too tight is a limiting factor, so early avoidance by screaming and frightening the mouse also has is merits. Of course, once farmer's wives gave up corsets the balance was restored.

The mousetrap is a much more fiendish invention. An intricate arrangement of straight pieces of wire, neat right angle bends and a coiled-up spring: perfectly balanced. But when a mouse with a long straight tail comes along string theory adds a subtle twist, literally. The spring has no choice but to become more tightly coiled. The slightest touch from the mouse and bang, all that energy is unleashed. It should be no surprise that when you take a mouse out of one of those traps its tail is often slightly curled.

You may feel sorry for the mice. You may feel that those straight tails are helping to keep your shoelaces tied. This is misplaced sympathy. They breed so fast that without farmers' wives and mousetraps we would be overrun. With so many straight tails around no knot would ever come untied. Try to imagine a world in which all knots were permanent. Christmas presents remain forever tied in ribbons, boats fail to leave harbour and we all have to wear slip-on shoes and wellingtons or risk dying with our boots on. Mice with their unnaturally straight tails are clearly plotting to upset the equilibrium of the universe. They deserve what they get.

Gordis Thriff - Introduction

Gordis Thriff is my alter ego—sort of. Skilled crossword addicts will recognise that his is an anagram of my name. This character was invented at the behest of a teacher on a creative writing course who wanted the group to dream up a character who was their opposite in as many ways as possible. Gordis is an unscrupulous con man, as nasty a self-serving miscreant as you would ever wish not to meet—except he came out funny.

My Granny's Jewels

It all started with my granny being robbed. Not a smooth con like an artist like me would pull off, oh no, some bloody amateur pretending to be a plumber. How hopeless is that.

The old biddy can't get about, so she lets him go off inspecting the house and he purloins the jewels. God knows why she let him in, it's not as though I haven't told her about that sort of thing. I should know, me the smoothest con artist you'll ever not realise you've been done by.

I've been visiting the old bat regular as clockwork; she never gave me a cent when I was a kid, no sweets, and no spare change like my mates all got from their grandmas. Those jewels, I've had my eyes on those jewels all my life, well since I was old enough to think about nicking them.

There's only me left; I'm her only relative so they're mine, except some boiler-suited bastard's walked off with them.

The old cripple didn't even know they'd gone, sleeps downstairs in a chair half the time, well all the time I think, only if you ask her she makes out she gets up to bed. Thing is the bed never looks like it's been slept in, so she can't fool me. If I hadn't told her they were missing, she still wouldn't have known they'd gone.

I should have taken them years ago, she'd never have known, but where's the art in that. They were going to be my honest jewels. That's hard to explain, coming from a con artist like me. I've never come by an honest thing in my life, but what I have lifted has all been skill. I've never been caught, dead smooth all the way. I do my home work, make all the false IDs, the proper paper work, the suits, the research, the skill, and then I get ripped off by some dirty fingernail with a greasy bag of tools for a trademark.

It's taken the joy out of it all. It's screwed me up. Everything feels pissed on. I don't know where to turn; it's not like I can go to some counselling course and say I feel professionally compromised and burned out because some fake plumber has hurt my pride. I have to tell someone, but where does a heartless hardened criminal bastard like me get therapy?

Con Artist

I hate the term con man. It just doesn't work does it, offends the old equal opportunity stuff, offends the ladies in the business and it sounds so down market. It did cross my mind to take someone to court; why shouldn't I be able to sue when this is just so sexist, but that's the problem in my game, who to sue?

Confidence trickster is just as bad; it implies that there's a trick to it, like some sort of magician. The work I do, and I do mean work, isn't a trick, some sort of quick flash of sleight of hand, it's a carefully executed plan worked out with all the details. It leads people to where they really wanted to go. A con only works if people want to believe it.

Con artist is the term, nothing else will do. What is art, some kind of trick of the light, some sort of illusion, could be a painting, a sculpture or a song, something that changes the mood, lifts the spirit? Everyone has their own idea about it; it's full of what they want to believe, full of connections to how they think the world ought to be. Full of stuff from the imagination; it's not real but we can't live without it.

You might think I'm being pretentious putting con artists up there with all that highbrow stuff but you're wrong. My job is to be a heartless bastard and without it society would be worse off. I have to deliver a high-class service; I'm not some sort of smash-and-grab man who just steals things, I ease people away from their money with a carefully planned illusion, a system of beliefs, a new way of looking at the world. Isn't that exactly what artists do? They lay on a performance, offer some sort of object that's not what it seems to be—and take your money.

There is one big difference between me and artists in the traditional sense: when you've paid for one of my performances you can get your money back from the insurance company. I think that's a better way of funding art than all this sponsorship nonsense, big corporations paying for damn great structures in public places. The policyholders, the customers of corporate bodies, pay it all for; the only difference is that my art is direct to the customer, one on one, real, memorable participation in the art itself. The customer is an integral part of the performance; in fact without the customer there would be no art. Con artist is the only word for it.

Customer Services

I had an interesting misfortune the other day. I was yet again travelling by train across the middle of England. I won't mention the name of the train company, no sense in asking for trouble. My fellow passengers and I had a totally new experience. The train stopped in the middle of nowhere. Not new, you may say, but then the PA system said that we were delayed by a train on fire coming the other way.

Exciting stuff, we were all agog to see this flaming wonder. As we waited it started to rain and in seconds we were in the middle of a major thunderstorm, complete with thunder and lightening.

There was still no sign of the burning train when the PA came back on to tell us that we would be delayed even longer because the signal box, somewhere up ahead, had been struck by lightening.

As an accomplished con artist who can dream up a line to fool anyone about anything, I can't say I was impressed. Given the flashes and bangs all around us no one could suggest that this was a very original line.

As we sat there in the countryside, watching the rain pelting down, I could see that my fellow passengers were taken in by this struck by lightening stuff. Fair enough, we were in the middle of a thunderstorm at the time, rain was crashing down and of course the train was stopped. We had a good view of the lightening.

That's the beauty of a good line, I thought, so long as if fits in with the grand scheme of things there's a good chance it will work. I remained calm, enjoyed watching the wild weather and waited.

We were told that because "the signals had been destroyed by lightning" we had to wait for a pilot man to come. Those were the exact words. I had thought we were on rails but it seems that sometimes they have to resort to something off the Mississippi, a pilot who knows the rapids or something like that. I guess he must have better vision or maybe a personal radar to spot trains coming the other way or some such.

After the pilot gets to us—which takes an hour or so, paddle steamers not being the fastest ships navigating the English countryside—and we are allowed to move on, we eventually get close to Oxford. Actually, we stop about 100 yards from the station and don't move.

Finally, I crack, and start hunting through the free magazine for a number to phone and dial up customer services. It's the usual stuff, press one for this two for that, so I go for the number that says customer services. It rings for a while and then I get a voice. I tell him how I am sitting on this train just outside Oxford, we are delayed 3 hours already so why are we still sitting still and what can he do about it? I am in the middle of telling him that I know for a fact that trains don't stop at Oxford for more than two minutes, so even if there is a train in front of us I can't see why we have been here for ten minutes already. He stops me right there.

'I'm sorry I can't help you, sir' he says, 'I am the man who books the helicopters for the Isles of Scilly, I don't deal with anything else.'

He offered to transfer me to another number but that turned out to be a recorded message.

I reflected on this before doing anything else. I had to admire their panache. What a line; it's so bizarre that anyone would think it must be true. It's what the propaganda merchants call the big lie; tell a story that is so preposterous that it must be true.

Suddenly, I am lost in admiration for the guys who run this railway; the quality of the training that goes into getting a customer service department that can come up with lines like the signals have been struck by lightning, or, I am just booking helicopters for the isles of Scilly. Top quality training. I had thought about going into the training business myself, there has to be a market for training from a high quality con artist, but now I have to think again, someone has beaten me to it.

Life in the Good Lane

Owing to a signalling problem we will be diverted into the goods lane. Doesn't sound too bad does it? But have you ever ordered goods, ever wondered why parcels don't arrive? Well now I know. I have travelled in the goods lane. Actually travelled may be a breach of the Trades Description Act, the word seems to imply motion, the getting of persons from place to place. Not today, sunshine.

Travel in the goods lane is a different experience, more akin to meditation. I have to thank one particular train company, who shall be nameless. I love the English countryside; the blend of different greens and browns, the occasional glimpse of wildlife. I appreciate the solidity of a stationary train, the calm, the silence, the lack of rumbling wheels and roaring engines. Life in the goods lane is good; presumably that's why they call them goods.

I realise now how important the goods lane is to the whole fabric of our life. Resting is so hard to achieve in today's hurly burly but the rail companies are doing their bit. Of course they have to show the timetable with the passenger trains in the express lane, the fast lane, because we are all told these days that we should be up there speeding along, but they don't call that the good lane.

So they do their bit, a signalling problem here, waiting for another train there, a medical problem last week, subtle, incomprehensible messages that no passenger can make real sense of, carefully disguising their real plan which is to get a little peace and calm back into our lives.

And when they can't get us into the goods lane what happens? Well for sure our parcels and letters go that way. When your delivery turns up late you should savour it, secure in the knowledge that your parcel, when it arrives, has been properly rested and is now calm, centred and ready to improve your life. Enjoy.

Patron Saint

St George slew a dragon; that must be some kind of a record, every body knows there never have been any dragons in this country, matter of fact there never have been any dragons anywhere at least not while people

34

have been around. There are no fossils, no remains, and no animals that look like descendants of dragons. There may have been the odd dinosaur hanging around Lyme Regis way, way back, and perhaps some of them had breath so bad it might have caught fire, but there weren't any people around then. No people fossils have popped out of the under cliff. There was no one to take notes or make up legends about dragons. So what the hell was St George up to? What did he slay?

My first instinct was always to admire the man; some heist it must be to convince a bunch of villagers that there was a dragon out there and then do it in. It's got to be one of the first ever cons, so you might think it would be on my list of all time greats. You have to wonder what he actually killed: was it a particularly dangerous cow or a bull even? It had to be something like that because there wasn't anything else around. How did he fake the fire breathing?

It sounds like a two-man con. He must have had a partner, there's no way even pretty gullible villagers are going to buy a story where some stranger on a horse turns up and announces that there's a fire-breathing dragon out there and he's going to go slay it for them. Not if they've never seen it themselves. What it needs is someone on the ground in the place beforehand that comes home with singed trousers a few times saying:

'Boy have I been lucky, only just got away from that thing.'

Of course it could be just kids playing with fire, that might work; George keeps a low profile, spots a kid being foolish and burning his fingers on something and says:

'Tell your mum it was the dragon and she'll let you off.' Kids are bound to fall for it; any way to get Mum off your back when you've been a bit silly with matches.

35

Of course first off Mum is just not going to believe it. Who would? Maybe if George managed to wind up a few kids he might have got something going. So he's certainly in the running to be the first ever con artist.

OK, the big question: if this guy is the first ever top class con, how come he ends up with his flag being painted on the heads of skinheads? That's a downer isn't it? The first and best con artist the county's ever seen is not going to end up being a legend for a bunch of hard nuts who've never fooled anyone about anything in their lives.

There really is only one explanation—it wasn't a con. I figure it went something like this. This George must have been some sort of Don Quixote figure, you remember the guy who ran around the country charging at windmills, well someone like that, and these villagers thought it would be fun to wind him up and set him to kill a cow, telling him it was a dragon. Maybe it was a bull he killed, but there again he wasn't Spanish like Don Quixote, so how could he have been a bullfighter?

So George kills the cow but how does it get dressed up as some sort of hero thing? He must have been the village idiot and some smartass set him up for a joke and then felt guilty about it. They must have felt sorry for him, so they put it about that he'd done a great deed, legendary stuff. That has to be it; who else would be the patron saint of skinheads except the village idiot.

36

Zombies - Introduction

I have heard numerous stories about Zombies and some of them can be particularly boring. I found the work from the Centre for Disease Control in the USA extremely refreshing. They were asked what preparedness had been done to deal with a Zombie Apocalypse. Other government agencies have been asked the same question and generally tend to produce answers that suggest that they are annoyed with people wasting their time. CDC, to their credit, rose to the task and used it as an opportunity to talk about disaster preparedness as a whole. They took it about as far as they could, producing among other things a 35-page comic novella, see: http://www.cdc.gov/phpr/zombies/#/page/1.

As a former medical academic and public health doctor, I was delighted to see this. I was similarly excited by Prof. Steven Schlozman's work describing what he calls *Ataxic Neurodegenerative Satiety Deficiency*. To translate that: ataxic means clumsy movements, neurodegenerative means that all or part of the nervous system including the brain are degenerating and satiety deficiency means that their hunger is never satisfied.

I have four zombie stories, which I hope are nothing like the ones I have heard or seen on TV. "Why Zombies Lurch" is my attempt at some sort of neurological explanation of their movement; the others are attempts to see an amusing side to Zombies.

My Dad Was a Zombie

My dad was a zombie. He was past middle age when it happened, so it didn't ruin his whole life. In the family, we tried not to make a big thing of it. Word got out eventually, and people did talk, and, worse still, the old fool encouraged them, doing the walk and all that.

He wasn't a zombie in the real sense, more fun-dead than un-dead. In the movie, you can barely make him out. He always claims he knows which one is him, but for the rest of us; well, you know, seen one zombie, seen them all. Distinctive personalities and looks are not really a zombie thing.

He kept the costume. My mum hated having it in the wardrobe, and you should have seen the face of the woman at the dry cleaners, but he wouldn't get rid of it. The bloodstains and gooey stuff were some sort of plastic bonded into the clothes, so whatever you did, it looked as bad as the first day he wore it.

We'd all heard the story a hundred times, and he almost had it out of his system, when some idiot suggested a re-union. It became a regular event; always on the last Tuesday before Halloween. You might think that was for some spooky reason, or because they'd blend in with all the students going to parties and such like. It was nothing so clever, just the anniversary of the day they made his scene in the film. All his mates, that had been extras like him, would dress up in their old gear and lurch around some pub or other that they'd hired for the night.

If I talk about my dad, everyone just remembers the zombie act. Given half a chance they'll start lurching around the room. It is amusing, and I do try to laugh, but there was a lot more to my dad than half an hour as a zombie extra, and I wish they'd remember that.

I still miss him. He always swore he'd come back as a real zombie. He said he'd had the training, knew all the moves, and was ready for the day. There were times when he was very convincing, as though he knew some secret, some crucial fact that everyone else has missed.

Every year, I go down the cemetery on the last Tuesday before Halloween … but he's never there.

Why Zombies Lurch

Zombies are the un-dead; OK, everyone has their problems, but why do they lurch? Whatever else you might think of them, lurching seems to be the characteristic gait. There exists a recognised taxonomy of movement disorders and it does not include lurching. In fact, there is an international society for movement disorders (http://www.movementdisorders.org) and a search of their web site gets no hits on lurching. Lurching is definitely non-human, so why do zombies do it?

The touch of zombies' flesh is chilling; they are at ambient temperature, cold, or even colder if they have only just come out of the ground. Is that any clue to the lurching?

Obviously much more research needs to be done on zombie metabolism, but given that the nerves, muscles and bones are all the same as they were, the basis of the lurching must lie in the nervous and musculoskeletal systems.

At lower temperatures, chemical reactions go slower. Reptiles can't move as fast when they are cold, because unlike mammals and birds, they can't regulate their body temperature. In that sense Zombies must be a bit like reptiles, and lets face it a lot of reptiles are somewhat creepy.

Muscles move because they are told to by nerve impulses, so if we want to understand lurching then we have to get to grips with the nervous system and how it works.

The nervous system is actually very complicated; it's not just one simple system, but layers of control and feedback superimposed on each other. No sense in going into too much detail, because I'd like the reader to remain awake, so lets start with the simple stuff. If you bang the big tendon below your kneecap with a rubber hammer, like doctors do, then your knee will jerk. The nerves that make that happen go from the tendon, to the spinal cord and then back to the muscles above the knee, and it all happens before the rest of the brain knows much about it. Further up the spinal cord, just inside the skull, is the cerebellum, and that co-ordinates movement. If it is damaged, then when you try to scratch your nose, you are just as likely to punch yourself in the eye.

Higher up the whole thing is the cerebral cortex, which is the bit that decides whether to scratch your nose at all. Under the cortex are other collections of cells that help coordinate movement, but cause problems like Parkinson's disease or Huntingdon's disease when they go wrong—not nice, but not actual zombie lurching.

One thing we do know is that these parts are all connected, and each influences the other. If you clench your teeth when you hit that knee tendon, then the jerk will be bigger and faster. Why? Because some of the extra nerve activity from the teeth clenching overflows down the spinal cord and gees up the whole system. Have you

40

ever noticed that if you grit your teeth you can lift a bigger weight? It's all part of the same thing, one part of the nervous system helping another.

Imagine all these messages whizzing up and down the nervous system, only slowed down a lot, because the zombie is running at ambient temperature rather than 37 Celsius. Nothing works the way it should. Those jerky lower reflexes have plenty of time to do their own thing before the rest of the nervous system finds out what is happening. When it does find out, the corrective messages take an age to arrive. The whole nervous system starts behaving like the British command at the charge of the light brigade, and the result is lurching.

Of course, that is not the whole story; Caribbean zombies, for instance, don't seem to lurch, they function much like anyone else, apart from being controlled by their masters. Caribbean zombies are controlled by voodoo, and that may be important.

In the Caribbean the higher temperature might stop them lurching, but they would be expected to rot so much faster that they'd be less of a threat. Zombies punching you is nasty; throwing their hand at you is not much fun either, but they are likely to miss and they can only do it twice, and after that they are armless—less likely to be harmful too. It is possible that the voodoo incorporates some means of slowing putrefaction. Clearly this is an important subject for further research.

The zombies we see on TV and in films inhabit cool climates and that appears to make lurching inevitable. It may be that they chase humans as much because they seek warmth as for food.

From this we can conclude an important lesson: make sure Zombies stay outside, do not let them loose in somewhere warm like a shopping mall or anywhere with central heating. If one, or even a group, traps you, the weapon of choice is a C02 fire extinguisher; the dry ice will cool them down, and they'll lurch to a standstill.

There is a risk, of course, that any wondering zombie will be taken to hospital, a nice warm environment. What would happen then? They would heat up and soon begin to achieve normal locomotion. Worse still, hospitals are the sort of places where finding a stray white coat or other disguise is rather too easy. If you happen to be in a hospital, talking to a doctor or being pushed on a trolley by a figure that looks at you with a vacant stare, don't hesitate; grab the fire extinguisher immediately.

How to Love a Zombie

Rule one: do not hold hands. You will only make that mistake once, because believe me, one-armed zombies are unattractive. Hugging and squeezing is out too; the last thing you need is extra goo coming out of places you didn't expect.

It is widely believed that some sort of viral infection creates zombies, and it's only right therefore to pay some attention to bio security. Zombies have a regrettable tendency to have bits drop off and to splash a certain amount of secretions around. Rule two, therefore, is: do not be tempted to collect the bits, even superglue won't stick them back on, they have no market value, and the zombie may not thank you for reminding them of their loss. The secretions, however, are easily avoided; Marigold gloves and Wellington boots and so on will do the trick—pick those coloured ones with flowers on, if you want the romantic look.

Now that we have the safety issues out of the way, it is probably sensible to pass on some counselling advice. Falling in love with zombies is rarely recommended. I'm not saying that out of some stereotypical prejudice; zombies are entitled to their bit of happiness, just as much as anyone else. It's just that it's easy to get hurt. Zombies are notoriously poor at showing their feelings, they rarely show affection, so whatever love you lavish on them may not be returned. Be warned. Take care.

Finally, there is the matter of kissing, and 'other exchanges of bodily fluids', as the chief medical officer puts it. Zombies are rather too free with bodily fluids, so the marigolds and wellingtons, with or without the flowers, may not be enough. Really, the answer is the internet; zombies, of all god's creatures, are made for cybersex.

Shy Zombie

People have no idea—well not just people, zombies have no idea either. I don't know who to talk to about it, or even how to talk about it. Why aren't there any zombie psychiatrists, or counsellors even?

I'm a zombie and I'm shy. There, I said it. That sounds a bit like shy anonymous.

Shy Anonymous, would that work? Would you want anyone to come? Like have adverts that say—we don't advertise 'cos we don't want anyone to come?

It wouldn't work for me though; I can't see anyone else staying if I came. Zombies have such a bad press; it's not fair, we have our problems too.

I've tried hard to get over it. I practice trying to, like, you know, be normal, moan, drool green slime, all the usual stuff. The trouble is practising on my own and doing it with others around isn't the same.

I've done all the nerdy things like trying to make a video diary, or trying to find someone to hook up with online. I don't know if you've noticed but for some reason zombies just don't go on the internet. I've tried the Skype and chat room things where you can find sort of random people to talk to, but they all just blank me.

I don't get it really, my web cam is dead cheap, so the picture's all pixelated, and I've set it to black and white so the purple green tinge doesn't show. I've even tried smearing Vaseline on the lens, like to blur it a bit, but it still doesn't work. I may have the world record for being blocked on the web. I read somewhere that cybersex works for zombies. Ha, well someone who never tried it wrote that.

It's all very well for humans, I mean they can do all sorts of stuff to get over being shy—like go to football or rock concerts, you know, places where everyone packs together and shouts about the same thing. I've watched them, well on TV, not up close. I can see how it works, they're all jammed together and the singing and the chanting and all that, well anyone would get over being shy wouldn't they. My trouble is zombies don't go to football matches and the one time I tried, well, lets just say it didn't go too well.

Other zombies don't seem to have my problem, they lurch around, crash into each other and drop bits of rotting flesh about the place and it doesn't bother them at all. I mean, they act like it doesn't matter, like everyone does it.

I find it all so embarrassing. Have they ever looked at themselves? There it is, that's my problem. I mean I don't know if I'm shy, or sensitive, or just have a better fashion sense than the rest of them. Deep down I know I'd have been so much better as a vampire. They have style; they're a much better class of un-dead. I wouldn't be shy if I was a vampire, well I don't think so, or maybe there are shy vampires too. No one would ever know would they, they're never going to get close enough to bite anyone. Forget about only going out at night, I mean, they'd probably never go out at all. Sad for them really lying in a coffin all day and night and never quite getting up the nerve to open the lid.

That's my problem—I see everyone else's point of view. It's no life, ha, life, what am I talking about, it's no existence for a zombie.

All the Other Stories

The remaining stories are mostly fictitious, or at least have some fiction within them. They are in that sense Not So, but they bear no relationship with Kipling or with the question answering style of the earlier stories. Some of the stories are based on real events; Hunt the Shoe, for example, was a real game, played for the first and only time at my daughter's birthday party. The Box in the Attic, was a real box in a real attic. Hairy Ape and There's a Lion Outside are based also on real events.

The Opera Murders

Live opera is food for the soul, but it requires dedication. My local opera house is old, and in the stalls below the circle, the only place I can afford to sit, the sound is terrible. Five rows in front of me, in clear air beyond the shadow of the circle, all the seats are taken by season ticket holders who have had them forever. They have a system, if you had a season ticket last year you get first refusal on keeping the seat next year—priority booking they call it. Once those seats are allocated you get the chance to bid for a better seat.

A year after I bought my season an elderly couple a row in front of me died, and I managed to move forward one row nearer to bliss.

Over the next two years, I suffered the agony of muffled arias and muted violins. How many more of those anonymous heads in front of me needed to die before I could get a seat in the pure sound zone? At least six, I calculated, but something nearer to a dozen would be more reliable. None of them looked ill.

I can't remember what took up the most time, finding their names and addresses, or researching ways to kill them so that every death was different. I knew that any hint of a common modus operandi might create suspicion. Every death had to look random and natural.

The first year, I moved forward two rows. Better, but not good enough. I killed seven the next year and moved forward two more rows, right to the edge of the dull zone. One more year, and I would be in clear air, with almost perfect sound.

Finding original ways to kill became so difficult that I only managed four more. I was astonishingly careful, obsessive about every detail, reverse engineering the forensics to throw off suspicion.

Thank God for opera, without that I might have freaked out completely. Two performances each month, even in my dull seat, kept me sane. It was so hard to go a whole year without putting a foot wrong, but I got my reward, two more rows forward and perfect acoustics. From that time on the uplift I felt after each concert was so great I was able to face the continuous hassle at work.

Every day I'd sit at my desk, surrounded by keen young detectives, full of enthusiasm and bright ideas. Today we are staring at a huge map with sixteen unexplained deaths.

'Tell me again.'

'Its some sort of revolutionary group, boss, with a grudge against toffs. The opera's the clue. Someone who hates opera has been killing them off. Look at the victims, they have one thing in common, they've all bought Opera CDs, season tickets to the opera house, trips to Covent Garden. They are all opera buffs. Someone hates them, but all the MOs are different, so it must be a group.'

47

'A revolutionary group bumping off opera lovers, that's your best guess? Any other signs of them? Any manifesto on the net? Have the spooks given us anything?'

'Not so far, boss.'

Now for the cunning bit. I paused a moment to be sure of every ounce of their attention.

'I commend your enthusiasm boys,' I said, 'but I can see weaknesses in your argument; that spending pattern, for example, it could be me. I've bought all of those things myself. I fit the victim profile.'

I scanned around the serious looking faces in front of me.

'You've done good work and it's a plausible story, no doubt about that, but there hasn't been a killing for two years. How do you account for that?'

'Maybe they think we're onto them.'

I folded the papers on my desk and closed the file.

'One thing for sure, boys, if you're right I'm obviously lucky to be alive.'

+ + +

Most of this story was written in my head in the years when my season ticket for the CBSO gave me a seat below the balcony in the old Birmingham Town Hall. Fortunately Sir Simon Rattle persuaded Birmingham to build Symphony Hall and from then on the audience enjoyed almost perfect acoustics. I changed the genre for the story to opera because I thought it fitted the plot, but I am forever grateful to Simon Rattle and the CBSO for the inspiring music that they made.

The Time Travel Paradox

We've all seen those adverts for genealogy services, where a modern character talks to their ancestors. Once time travel was invented, reality caught up with advertising. It became a new kind of reality TV. I jumped at the chance to take part.

Before they started filming, they searched through the archives, piecing together my family tree, trying to find the most important time zone to actually visit. They gave me some indoctrination about what they called the time travel paradox. You can't meet yourself, and you must not upset history.

The script said to observe, pretend it was educational and bring history alive.

That was the plan.

In my case interest soon focused on James Alsop Brown. This man appeared to have squandered an enormous fortune, destroying his family and leaving a destitute son from whom I was descended a mere five generations later.

There had been lands and great houses as well as records of vast sums in the banks, but every last penny was gone.

Most went on one madcap adventure, trying to find Shangri-La. Everyone knows the myth. The producers couldn't resist showing clips of that old movie, "Lost Horizon", just to add background, they said.

To anyone with a modicum of intelligence the idea of a hidden valley somewhere in the Himalayas where people live forever is obvious nonsense. The population would soon grow to the point where there could not possibly be enough food. The story cannot possibly be true, but my ancestor was fooled into thinking he could find the place.

He didn't just mount one expedition; he kept doing it. He paid vast sums to suspicious characters that claimed to know the way. He paid for equipment and provisions for one expedition after another. Between these ventures, there was some evidence that he drank as though there was no tomorrow, but mostly the fortune went on searching for Shangri-La. Instead of living forever, he died young and poor.

After careful research we settled upon a short period between his expeditions where we had some certainty as to where he would be, with a good chance that he could be observed without arousing suspicion. He frequented a particular club where I hoped to be able to see him and hear him talk to other members, so that I could understand why he was so set on this hopeless task.

On the TV programme, this came down to a few minutes of screen time, but in reality, I spent many days sitting in a green leather armchair at that club, reading newspapers, drinking tea, and listening to interminable conversations among rich young aristocrats. By the end of it, I was beginning to be glad that James's crazy expeditions extracted my ancestors from that particular social set. Unfortunately, all I discovered was the depth of his obsession. All his friends and acquaintances thought he was insane, and some told him so, but nothing changed his determination to mount another expedition.

The next plan was to go back to a time before the first venture. That got nowhere. In frustration I even risked actually talking to him. I had to disguise myself and shake off minders from the programme. I asked him what he thought of stories about Shangri-La. He told me to my face that he thought it was a ridiculous notion. He laughed at me. This man who was about to spend his entire life and my family's fortune on a madcap idea, laughed at me for suggesting it.

If I have inherited anything from him, I suspect it may be a tendency to become obsessional once something is in my head. I should have simply gone back to my own time and forgotten all about it, but his laughter made me angry.

The man must be lying. Of course he had no way of knowing that I was his descendent and that he had ruined the family and caused dreadful hardship, but I felt that he was insulting me and all the generations that lay between us.

In my fury I resolved to kill him, hang the rules, I thought, this man has to die.

I purchased a blunderbuss. I did consider a bow and arrow or a crossbow, but that would take hours of practice. A sword or a dagger would mean getting too close, but I found a place where I was sure I could hide, so that I could shoot him as he took his regular evening walk.

I tried a few practice shots in secluded places until I was sure I could hold the gun steady and not flinch at the fearsome noise it made. I lay in wait and at exactly the right moment, I pulled the trigger. I felt the weapon jerk and a blast of shot and smoke belched towards him. As the air cleared, I saw him still walking, oblivious to the sound and untouched by the missiles that had appeared to envelope him.

As I watched, he put his hand to his brow and stopped in his tracks. He stood for several minutes, lost in thought, and then hurried off towards his front door.

I felt the gun, the barrel was hot; there was no question that it had fired. I inspected the trees nearby and found pieces of shot. It made no sense; until the thought dawned on me that there must be some law of the universe that prevented me from killing an ancestor. If I had killed him then I could not have been born, and so I could not kill him.

But that was not the worst of it.

Over the next few weeks, the full horror of the time travel paradox emerged. He began to tell his friends of a terrible experience he had suffered. A profound feeling had descended on him, as though someone had walked over his grave.

'Not just walked on it, old boy, bloody jumped up and down,' he'd say. 'Made me feel dreadful right down to my boots, chilled my very soul. It made me sure that I'm not long for this life.'

From this near death experience came his obsession with Shangri-La.

'Some chap told me about it a few weeks back. Don't know his name, never seen him before. I laughed at him, told him he was crazy, but after that turn the other night, I just know I have to find it. If it costs me every penny I own, I have to find it.'

You Will Meet a Tall Dark Stranger

'You will meet a tall dark stranger.'

I can't believe I'm doing this. She actually has a crystal ball, or at least a glass thing that I can't see into because it's so bloody dark in here. Can she see anything, I wonder?

'Isn't that what gypsies always say?'

'Who are you calling a gypsy?'

I took a deep breath; this was definitely a mistake.

'There's a sign outside your door, "Gypsy Nell", I thought that was a clue.'

That ought to slow her up I thought. I should never have agreed to this. Ten minutes to change your life the poster said, and all she can manage is the tall dark stranger bit. What a joke, Gypsy Nell.

'Oh that, she says, nothing to do with me, that's the bloke that runs the circus, I think it's left over from the last lady.'

'What happened did she see something in the glass that made her do a runner?'

I thought that was clever of me, I mean, I've always wondered why all fortune-tellers aren't super rich. If you can see the future, why would you end up with a crummy job in some itinerant circus?

'Something like that,' she says. 'She disappeared and the police turned up the next day.'

'She sounds like the sort of woman I should see, do you know where she went?'

'I'm not supposed to say.'

There was a hint of strain in her voice and I suddenly felt sorry for her.

'It must be bad for your eyes working in this dim light all day,' I said. 'Don't you get headaches or eye strain?'

'Tell me about it,' she says, taking her eyes off the crystal ball for a moment. 'I only started last week, I'm a trapeze artist myself, high wire stuff, but the ring master thought it would be good to work in a dim light for a while, make it easier to see the ropes and bars up there in the big top. You know sometimes the light is very variable and people take flash photos and all that. It's all very well having good hands and being fit, but if you can't see the catch, you're in the net whatever.'

'I hope you can't see yourself falling off, in that ball thing, that would be awful and so much pressure.'

She sat back, looking up at me for the first time.

'That's the first nice thing anyone has said to me all week,' she said. 'You can't believe what a dumb job this is. Half the people that come in are drunk and their mates have egged them on. The rest either want the lottery numbers or to know if their husband's cheating on them.'

'How awful,' I said. 'So do any of them go out happy?'

'I try to tell them, about the lottery,' she said. 'I can't give the numbers to everyone or there would be so many winners they'd all end up with four pence. I try to make out it's a sort of fortune teller's ethics thing, you know, like we have a deal with the lottery not to let on.'

'What do you do about the husband question?'

'What would you do? I figure, if they've asked then he probably is cheating. I tell them they have a choice. Me telling them won't count as evidence, so if they want to go to court they'll have to hire a detective, or they can put up with him, or confront him. Either way I don't want some irate husband coming in here.'

'Because you can't see it in the stars.'

'Dead bloody right.'

So now I know, this is definitely a con, should have come last week when the other woman was here.

'You could always run away up the high wire, they wouldn't follow up there.'

'Yeah, sure, but I'd have to come down again, they don't do meals up there.'

I laughed, somehow I was beginning to like this girl. The noise outside the tent had gone and I guessed my mates must have gone for that drink.

'Are you sure you don't have the number for the other lady?'

She smiled. 'Oh well, for a mate,' she said. Hang on a sec.' She got up and rummaged in a bag at the back of the tent, picked up a pencil and wrote on a scrap of blue paper. 'She may not still be there.'

'I'll take the chance,' I said. 'Thanks I've really enjoyed the session.'

It took me two days to get around to finding the address and getting up the nerve to go and ring the bell. I stood there clutching the scrap of blue paper. A tall dark strange woman opened the door, looked me up and down and smiled.

'Come in,' she said. 'I was expecting you.'

She told my fortune, for an exorbitant fee and, of course, it was complete rubbish. I worked it out eventually. The whole thing was an elaborate con; the scrap of blue paper was the code; I imagine they split the fees.

The Six Fifteen from New Street

Whilst daydreaming in a queue at the bank I saw a scrap of paper on the floor, a couple of inches across and folded with part of a footprint in one corner. Should I pick it up?

I'm in a bank; it might have important information on it but if I pick it up will it look suspicious? What if it has account numbers on it?

I'm at the front of the queue, a transition point, a place where life-changing events happen, where I may cease to be in queuing limbo and become a customer. If I try to pick up the paper, I am bound to be called forward while I'm grovelling on the floor. I could look foolish; everyone behind me will think I am holding up the queue. I'll leave it.

"You've dropped a piece of paper," says a voice behind me; interesting accent, Italian maybe?

Everything changes, now I have a reason to pick it up. If I do, I am implying that it's mine, which is a deceit of sorts, effectively lying to the woman behind me. Hardly a major crime, at least not yet, but any action will be caught on the security cameras for sure. I could say it's not mine, but I am curious.

I glance at the counter. The old lady is still talking to the teller and it sounds like it could go on a while.

I bend down to pick up the paper.

Should I read it?

No, no, says a small voice in my head, James Bond would not fall for that one. If it is mine then I must already know what it is. I keep up the act, put it in my pocket, smile at the woman behind and say thanks.

Now the old lady is done talking to the teller and is putting papers in her bag. I step up to the counter and pay my money in.

The piece of paper is beginning to burn a hole in my pocket. My curiosity is rising, so I stroll as nonchalantly as I can out of the bank. I can feel my hand wanting to grab the paper. I'm tempted to look behind me in case the Italian woman is there, but Bulldog Drummond wouldn't fall for that. In my mind I'm carrying some crucial secret message—the future of the free world hanging on not being discovered.

Outside the bank my way is temporarily blocked by a bunch of lads wearing camouflage kit. I have a fleeting thought that they might be troops about to grab my secret paper, but they're too young.

Why is that camo fabric so fashionable? I'm tempted to walk straight ahead and collide spectacularly with one of them and say, "Oh sorry, gosh you're well camouflaged." But they are all bigger than me, so I'll save the joke for another day.

Coffee, that's the answer. I step around the pretend soldiers. There's a Costa just down the street; I've got their loyalty card so why not show a spot of loyalty right now.

I order a latte and find a seat in a dim corner, settle myself, take my iPad out of my bag and dig the paper out of my pocket, trying to look as though it's some sort of reminder I wrote myself earlier.

I open the folded paper. That footprint on one corner must have been wet once, the paper has obviously been soggy and it has now dried out and stuck together. Trying to look relaxed, I tease it apart.

It says 6.15 from New Street. Block capitals. Obviously carefully written by someone who didn't want to make a mistake.

At least it's not a bank account or something vital like that, and surely it's too short to be some secret code.

Other possibilities flash into my mind, a lovers tryst perhaps, a secret meeting. What if the person who wrote it never gets there? Awful thought, but wait a moment—it says 6.15 FROM New Street, it's not about meeting a train, it's catching a train, or being on a train. Where does the 6.15 go to? Lucky I have the iPad. Five minutes research tells me the 6.15 goes to Edinburgh, via Warrington. It could of course be the local train to Four Oaks, but those little trains are late half of the time, no one could be making precise notes about anything as unreliable as that.

Edinburgh is romantic, but doesn't make sense. I'm in Worcester, the exact opposite direction from New Street. Why would someone make a careful note of a train that goes to Scotland and then leave it in a bank in Worcester.

Maybe they're planning to catch the train? I hope they don't miss it. By now my coffee is cold and my head is full of possibilities, everything from Brief Encounter to Murder on The Orient Express.

Wait a minute, there's something else, under the footprint; I almost lost it getting the fold apart. There's just a few letters, another clue. I smooth it out with my fingernail, trying to appear like a harmless obsessive.

Sandra, it says. So, Sandra is going to be on the 6.15, but whoever wrote the note might not be there.

She may be upset. All kinds of tragedies race through my mind; is there any way to get a message to her? What does Sandra look like? Is there a face type for Sandra. Do parents take one look at a newborn baby and think, that's a Sandra if ever I saw one.

Another search on the iPad throws up fifty Sandra pictures and a lot of them do look very similar, alike even. I'm onto something here, and then it dawns, they're all Sandra Bullock. Images of Gravity and the Oscars fly through my mind.

The hell with it, I'm not cut out to be a spy. I scrunch up the paper and leave it to go soggy in the remains of my coffee. I hope Sandra doesn't get lonely in Scotland.

It Was a Dark and Stormy Night

All that could be seen in the dark cellar was a small window and a single shaft of moonlight.

'We're in trouble now.'
'Why?'
'Look at that—we're stuck in a cliché.'
'You mean one of those phrases that used to be good, but has been used too often?'

'Exactly. How many stories have you read with a cellar and a single shaft of moonlight?'

'It's the single shaft that does it.'

'A pool of moonlight on the floor would have been just as bad.'

'You mean like a dark and stormy night?'

'Yes.'

'But it <u>is</u> a dark and stormy night. That's why we came in here.'

'But it's too dark to find a way out.'

Long pause.

'There must be some way out of here—'

'Said the joker to the thief.'

'What?'

'It's a Bob Dylan song. All Along the Watchtower.'

'There isn't a watchtower.'

'But it's still a cliché.'

The whole cellar is lit up as a bolt of lightening crashes outside.

'Through the mad mystic hammering of the wild ripping hail, the sky cracked its poems in naked wonder.'

'Very poetic, isn't that Bob Dylan too?'

'Yeah, but it's not a cliché, no-one else uses it.'

'So?'

'So it's the Chimes of Freedom.'

'You've lost me.'

'Just listen for the chimes of that grandfather clock in the hall. It's right by the front door. Stand under that and we'll get our bearings, we'll know exactly where we are.'

A Quiet Life

Heavy clay, he thought as the spade dug through the turf, just my luck. He straightened his back; not as bad as prison anyway. Sweat blurred his vision as he waved at the splash of colour that was Joyce on a deckchair. Another day, another favour. He turned the next sod and watched a drip of sweat fall. You're just a friendly face with no willpower, his mother had said a hundred times.

Years ago he'd thought his face was his fortune; people believed him, believed anything he said. He could con anyone, except the judge of course.

Jail killed his confidence and he couldn't con a rabbit, but his face still made him approachable, and everyone thought they could ask him anything. He couldn't say no. He could see it in their eyes, that friendly face would never say no.

He plunged the spade in again, turned another sod and tried not to look at Joyce. A neighbour with a broken leg, and he was a sucker for a helpless woman. He knew where that came from; seeing his mum bleeding, when dad was drunk. Keep digging. The spade hit something solid. He wrestled with the spade for a moment and revealed a small metal box. Another twist bent the lid and jewels gleamed in the sun.

He knelt beside the hole; his fingers touched the cold stones. He glanced at Joyce, no sign of movement.

'Just my luck, but who will believe me,' he thought.

Still stooping, he tipped the compost into the hole and planted the small apple tree. He stood up holding the tree upright.

'OK here?' he called to Joyce. She waved.

He firmed the ground with his boot.

'Anything for a quiet life,' he muttered, and hoped the promised beer was still cold.

Another Man's Arm

She was a pretty girl, not a devastating Hollywood beauty, just one of those rare people that have a glow. She had dark sparkling eyes that grabbed your attention, a quick smile, a slim nose, and the way she moved was a delight. Add to that a transparent air of innocence and you can see why every eye followed her.

If you work in Casualty a long time it's easy to notice that the nurses are sometimes put off by really pretty girls, or maybe they just notice the impact that they have on the male doctors. There was none of that, this girl's charm worked on everyone. She sauntered over to me and I was so taken with her that I hardly noticed that she was holding a man's arm.

It must have been half a minute before it occurred to me to think:

"Whose arm is that? Where did she get it? How did she get it?"

She carefully placed the arm on the table and looked directly at me.

'Can you fix it?'

'You mean re-attach the arm?'

'Yes,' she said, 'I've kept it cool, it's been on ice in the car.'

'Where is the casualty?'

'The casualty?'

'The man who has lost the arm.'

'I don't understand,' she said.

This was becoming more complicated.

61

'We may be able to re-attach the arm,' I said, trying to be professional and not sound irritated, 'but we need to see the other side of the wound. Is he in an ambulance on his way here?'

She still looked at me with a puzzled, though very charming smile.

'Can't you do it with stem cells?'

It was my turn to look blank.

'I thought you could grow a new one with stem calls,' she said.

'You mean grow back the rest of the person?'

'Yes,' she said. 'I brought this in case it was needed.'

She heaved a half gallon plastic can out of her bag.

'It's not all of the blood, but it's all I could get. There may be some crunched up bone in it too, that has stem cells doesn't it. With that, and the ones in the arm, that should be enough surely?'

I must have looked blank.

'I thought it was a good idea in case.'

'In case of what?'

'In case you need more stem cells. I wasn't sure if there would be any in the hamburgers.'

Now I was really lost.

'What have hamburgers got to do with it?'

'He fell into the hamburger machine. He was very curious about everything, always trying things.'

For a moment her sunny expression clouded.

'I told him not to, I kept telling him, but he never listened. Perhaps if we can grow a new one onto his arm I can train him better.'

I knew I was getting into something deep here but somehow I couldn't stop.

'Can I get something clear,' I said. 'You are saying that the owner of this arm, your boyfriend or whoever he was, fell into a hamburger machine.'

'Yes,' she said. 'I grabbed at him to try to pull him out and all I got was his arm. I couldn't stop the machine so I tried to save all the blood before I washed it out.'

'You washed it out?'

'Well yes, I couldn't leave it like that, it's unhygienic.'

'So all that's left of him is this arm?'

'Yes, and the blood,' she paused looking at me with that innocent, appealing smile.

'Ah, yes,' I said, 'and the blood. Have you told the police?'

'Why? Can they do stem cells?'

'No,' I said. 'They do forensics. They investigate crimes.'

'What crime?'

'The death of the owner of this arm.'

'But he's not dead, the arm is fine, that's why I brought it, so you could grow him back.'

'Some people might call that dead,' I said, 'and they might think you killed him.'

She turned that ice melting smile on me again.

'No,' she said. 'I was trying to save him, that's why I brought the arm.'

'And the blood,' I said.

'Yes,' she said. 'And the blood.'

'I need to make some phone calls,' I said. 'I'll just get one of the nurses to put the arm and the blood in the fridge. You wait here, OK?'

'Do you want the hamburgers too?'

'The hamburgers? You kept the hamburgers?'

'Of course.'

'How many.'

63

'About five hundred quarter pounders, they're in the car, I wasn't sure if you'd need them.'

This was getting past a joke. I tried to think what the police would ask me when I phoned.

'What happened to the bones?'

For a moment she looked embarrassed.

'I think most of them just got crushed up, but there may be some bits in the hamburgers.'

She looked at me carefully for a moment.

'That white coat—you are a doctor aren't you, not a food inspector?' For a moment her beautiful smile clouded. 'I wasn't going to sell the burgers, honest, they just come out of the machine like that.'

'No, of course not,' I said, still thinking about what to say to the cops. 'You'd never get away with it, they test hamburgers for DNA these days.'

Buried

The JCB made slow progress over the dunes. Even with the caterpillar tracks, it would slew around unexpectedly. The onlookers leapt back, thinking it might fall over, and they had a bad time keeping their feet on the shifting sand. The single uniformed constable struggled. Shouting ineffectually over the din of the engine and desperate to avoid falling over and looking foolish, he achieved almost nothing. As fast as he told people to keep back, someone else would appear in a new vantage point and start filming events on their phone. It was only a matter of time before the press arrived and proper TV cameras on tripods began to record the scene.

Once the professionals were on hand, attention focused on the little boy holding the hand of a man who appeared to be directing operations. Leaning over to talk to the child, the man signalled to the JCB driver who stopped, dropped his jacks into position and began digging. It was a slow process. As fast as sand was removed more slid back to fill the hole. The machine scooped out a bucket full of sand and then swung around to deposit it yards away. The crowd were forced back by the rotations of the machine so that it was harder to see into the hole.

After a few minutes, the diver got out of the cab and came over to talk to the man and the boy. Against the noise of the machine, the crowd could hear nothing but by now the reporters knew they were on to something.

'Can we have a live feed?'

The cameraman laughed. 'How often have you wanted to say that?'

The reporter took no notice, turned away from the noise and carried on speaking.

'There's something going on. There's a kid here with detective Roberts from the local nick. They're digging for something. We can give you pictures from here but someone better call the front desk and see if they can get any background.'

They say that relationships between the press and police are too close, so much so that both are now suspicious of each other; but open up the possibility of being on the national news with a major crime and it's a different story. The news desk and the reporter were overcome with excitement and an animated and confused conversation ensued.

'This kid says his mummy is buried.'

'You mean he just pitched up at the station with a story like that and you believed him?'

'No, he told his teacher and she quizzed him a lot before she took it seriously.'

'What does his father say?'

'Some cock and bull story that the mother's swimming the channel. Says they've been down here the last three weeks to practice.'

The reporter put the phone down and started hitting search engines. People who swim the channel do it for a reason; they raise money for charity, they seek publicity, someone must know. Half an hour searching had turned up no sponsors, no money, no publicity, and no sign of anyone setting off from England to swim the channel. No one swims the channel for fun; maybe the kid is right, mummy is buried.

By now the story had got to the producer for the evening news, and, it being a slow news day, arrangements had been made to feed direct to London. The possibility of a body being dug up live on national TV was impossible to turn down.

Back at the beach, more uniforms had arrived and were trying to fence off the area with red and white police tape. A thankless task as the wind was getting up and the stakes they had brought wouldn't hold in the sand.

The crowd grew as word got around among the holidaymakers braving the weather. This was much more entertaining than trying to convince themselves that they were enjoying the seaside.

The JCB delved deeper and the piles of sand that had been removed were building up like a parapet around the digger. A senior policeman muttered to a colleague,

'There's no way we can get a tent in place on this, we'd need a bloody marquee, and then it would blow away. When they get down to the body I want all the uniforms around in a circle and we'd better have a stretcher from an ambulance or something, with a big cloth to go over the whole thing.'

'She'll be in once piece, do you reckon, Sarge?'

'Don't let your imagination run wild, sunshine. She was seen at the hotel two days ago, she ain't had time to rot if that's what you're thinking.'

'Just think about that poor kid seeing his mummy being buried, I mean he must have seen mustn't he, 'cos he knows where to dig.'

Another constable came over.

'We've had it with the tape, Sarge, can't get anything to hold in the wind.'

'No worries, Bob. Go and have a word with our man on the JCB and see if he can pile the sand all the way round, make a bit of a barrier. Are forensics and the pathologist ready to move?'

'All set, Sarge.'

'Right, get everyone in position, can't do anything about those cameras, with their lenses they'll tell us what nail varnish she's wearing from half a mile away, but we can keep out Joe Public. Anyone who gets in the way, arrest them for interfering with police work. Smith, is the husband here? Get him out of the car, I want to see his face when the digging stops.'

And so it was that a few minutes after six, live on three TV channels at once a small boy rushed forward, eluding his detective minder, narrowly avoiding the JCB bucket, and almost falling headlong into the hole, emerged triumphantly holding a six inch long plastic mummy.

Minutes later the French TV cameras arrived to film the boy's mother emerging from the sea.

'What the hell do we do now, Sarge?'

'Grab the father and son, form a guard of honour, down to the beach on the double.'

'What's your name?'

'Catch.'

'That's a weird name for a kid.'

'Well that's what they all say when they throw things at me.'

'What do they throw?'

'Rocks mostly, crusts or something I can eat if I'm lucky.'

The kid grinned, ducked his head and squirmed away, but the big man was too quick for him and grabbed his coat. Before he could wriggle out of it, he had an arm and then one huge hand was grasping his shoulder.

'Not so fast, we haven't finished.' Twisting him around, the dark brown eyes searched his face. 'Do you have another name?'

'Don't know.'

'I've got more questions, are you gonna run some more?'

The kid looked up, his glance darting between the figure in front of him and the nearest building. He shrugged; it was too far away, he'd never make it. The hand on his shoulder relaxed a little, but didn't move.

'This way, kid.'

Three steps took them to the car and the kid climbed in with startling alacrity, bouncing on the seat.

'Have you ever been in one of these?'.

'Cop car init?'

'Sure is.'

'Am I going to jail?'

'Not unless you can drive this thing.'

'How thick are you? I'm sitting in the back seat, even a big bugger like you can't reach the pedals from here.'

The kid stopped looking at the controls for a second and risked a glance at the man alongside him, grinning, raising his eyebrow a fraction. Sensing the attention on his face, his right hand sneaked across to the door handle and pressed it. His body tensed to jump and run; he pushed harder, then sank back in the seat defeated.

'I can't get out can I.'

'Not unless you can jump over a big bugger like me.'

The smile came back.

'Where do you live?'

'Like a house, you mean?'

'With your mum or your dad.'

'Fifty-two Newbold Road.'

The big man leaned forward and touched the driver on the shoulder

'Did you get that?'

The driver half turned.

'There's only forty houses in Newbold Road.'

'Try another one, kid.'

'Catch. Catch is my name, not kid.'

'OK, Catch, have you got a last name.'

'Little Thief.'

The detective laughed. 'That's the other thing they call you, huh. How long have you lived on the streets?'

'I don't live on the street.'

'Kid, either you live in a house or you live on the street.'

'I live under the street.'

'Have you always been this smart, Catch? Nah, don't answer that one, how would you know. Any idea how old you are?'

'I might be twelve, or maybe thirteen.'

'Did you go to school?'

'Before my mum died.'

69

'When was that?'

The kid shrugged.

'Well, roughly, like how many winters ago?'

'I'm not a Red Indian.'

'I never said you were.'

'Then don't make with the how many moons stuff. It was the seventh of January 2007, why does it matter?'

'You've been on your own since then?'

'Mostly. Sometimes I hang out with people.'

'Who?'

'Whoever, I'm a little thief remember. I go with anyone I can get stuff from.'

'So I should arrest you for stealing?'

'Not that kind of stuff.'

'What then?'

'Learning, brain stuff, finding things out. Reading, computers, money, languages, stuff to know, good stuff.' For a second there was another flash of a smile, captivating, enticing. 'I can't go to school, they'd have me in an orphanage and I'd never get out or learn anything either.'

'That's not how it is, Catch.'

'They don't teach cops much do they?'

'Meaning what?'

'Do you know how many GCSEs the average kid in care gets? Do you know what percentage of kids in care end up in jail? Put me in there and I'll end up being a top gang leader in ten years time and give you loads of trouble. I'll have to change my name of course.'

'Because we'll never catch you?'

The mercurial smile flashed across his face again.

'On the other hand we could say I'm sixteen and small for my age and I could help you. Pretty soon they'd be calling you Catch. What do you reckon?'

Cream Cake

The church clock struck noon so loudly it might have woken the dead; maybe that's the idea. One minute I'd just bought my cream cake and the next second; bong, bong, bong and I have a screaming baby. Twelve great bongs and he couldn't have been more awake if he'd sat on a pin.

It only lasted a minute. Most people were walking by as if nothing happened but little Alfie wouldn't stop. There I was in a busy high street with everyone looking at me as though I'm the worst mother in the world. There are two kinds of looks. There are the honest disapproving kind that look straight at you, frowning and at the same time doing body language that says they could do it better. I can cope with them because I know deep down that they would do no better. The ones I hate are those that look the other way, or even cross the road, pointedly, not having the nerve to show their feelings to my face.

I've seen three of the first kind and two of the others when the vicar comes along and gives me that oh so sympathetic, but holier than thou look. The nerve of the man, it's his bloody church bells after all.

'Can I help?' he said, all descending from on high to help the poor and afflicted.

'Yes you can,' I said.

I resisted the temptation to hit him in the face with the cake. OK it would be satisfying, but I'd have no cake.

'Can you mind the pram for a second?' I said. I rushed into the shop and bought another cake, a big one oozing cream.

'There is one more thing you could do,' I said.

'Bless you, of course I'll help,' he says.

'Stand still,' I said, and hit him right in the face with the cream cake.

Hairy Ape

I don't know why calling someone a hairy ape is supposed to be an insult, I mean, surely we are all hairy apes, apart from some friends of mine that have spent a fortune on laser treatments.

People said it about John, which was sort of understandable because he was about six foot five and broad shouldered and he had a beard. On the other hand, if you'd have to guess, without having done any biology at school, you'd have thought he was a bear rather than an ape.

He was actually a shy gentle soul, and just like gorillas he was a vegetarian. That's where the resemblance ended; I never saw John beating on his chest to scare people off and he cooked his food rather than tearing off raw shoots. He was huge though, I mean if you spent a lot of time with him there was no danger of getting suntanned.

I remember once when we were in China three of us were walking down a street, John in the middle and me and Jeanette either side, which I suppose made him seem even bigger, and I saw something I've never seen before.

I should say that we were deep in China, over towards Chengdu and there were not many Europeans in those parts back then. Wherever we went we got attention, kids running behind us in the street waving and shouting to their friends and that sort of thing. We came around a corner of a building and suddenly in front of us was this little Chinese man, I guess he was about five foot three. I'm not being heightist here, I mean lots of the Chinese people were small by European standards, in a crowd I could see where I was going, so this old man must have thought John was a giant.

He was a live copy of caricature Chinaman, you know wearing one of those jacket and trouser things that look like denim pyjamas. His jaw dropped.

I've read that expression a few times; they say it in magazines don't they, well at least they do in some of the ones I read, but I'd never seen it for real. It really did look as though the poor man had some sudden paralysis in his muscles, as though his chin might fall off. He was stranded there, stopped in his tracks with his mouth open so wide that some passing insect could have flown in and invited all its relatives to follow.

The little Chinese fellow looked about seventy and I don't think he'd ever seen a westerner before, let alone anyone like John. It was one of those moments that seem to go on forever, though really it was about five seconds. I never realised before where that jaw drop expression came from; now every time I read it I see the hairy ape and the little Chinese man.

Phrases like that have to come from somewhere I suppose; I mean the first person that saw a dropped jaw must have thought, "Hey look at that—I'll use that."

Does it make it more likely to happen I wonder, you know, using the words? Does it get it into people's heads so that they know your jaw is supposed to drop if you are shocked? Words have power don't they. Since I had that thought I've been more careful how I talk. I mean, "hairy ape" may be safe enough, because, like I said, we all are aren't we; but for instance I used to say "drop dead gorgeous" a lot, well not any more.

Hunt the Shoe

A birthday party for six year olds, how hard can it be? It's just food and games, right? The food was easy, but what I wasn't ready for was the fantastic energy of fifteen six year olds.

Most of the games, whatever the rules might have said, involved running around screaming, or on occasions screaming and running around. The noise was deafening. Each game took far less time than I expected, and even with a break for food, I realised that I would run out of games well before any of them would be taken off my hands. I had to invent a new game, and preferably one that would take at least half an hour to play.

Under such circumstances, it's hard to see the thing through completely, to guess the possible snags. There's no time for practice runs. The crucial elements of the game needed to be that everyone was involved; that there was an element of competition and that it should take at least twenty minutes. I think 'Hunt the Shoe' has only ever been played once.

It goes like this. All the kids take off their shoes, I run around the house hiding them, and the first one to find both their shoes is the winner. What could be simpler? I left them scoffing the last of the food while I found relatively easy hiding places. Once back, I set them loose.

The usual rushing and screaming followed, but thankfully, being spread over the whole house diluted the noise. About a quarter of an hour had gone by before I began to think that it was taking them a long time. I started strolling around the house to see how things were going. There were of course six year olds rushing around my feet and I had to make sure that they couldn't see where I was looking. Several of them were clutching one shoe, so progress was obviously being made.

After about twenty minutes, I spotted what was happening. All of them were at it. If they found someone else's shoe, they re-hid it, but often in a new place. All over the house, shoes were moving around, and gradually being hidden in increasingly fiendish places. I had completely underestimated the mischievous intelligence of six year olds.

Round about then the first parent arrived to collect their offspring, who, as one might expect was clutching one shoe and tearing around the house with the rest of them. We made small talk for a while, until the second parent turned up, and then the third. Still no one had won, and what was more, I had no idea where any of the shoes were.

At that point, we had to change the rules. The prize goes to whoever can find the most shoes. A large pile soon accumulated, but the phrase 'Whose shoes are these?' still fills me with a sort of horror.

I Was Here Before

I think it is something to do with the temporal lobe, those bits of the brain that, surprisingly enough, lie behind the temples. Over activity there gives the feeling of dejá vue. Seen before, if you translate it into English, been before, if you go on how it feels. How can you tell if it is an illusion or not?

It depends a bit on where it happens; if I go to a place I've never been before and get an attack of dejá vue then I can be pretty sure that it's my brain fooling me. Often there is a deeper impression, not just of having seen before, but smells, feelings, the whole bag. To a very rational person that might provide a bit of a clue. How likely is it that if I went back to some place, that I'd have the same mood and feelings? I might well remember how I felt, but that's never the same as actually feeling the same.

To a less rational person it's more spooky, mostly because all of those feelings create a much more convincing impression of reality. So what does the imagination do? If you know for sure you've never been in Texas, or Berlin, or wherever before, then it must have been in a former life.

From there on the psyche is on a free ride to never land. It's very easy to imagine cues in everyday life as clues to former existence: a tree that seems familiar, a curve in the road, a funny-shaped cloud, the sky at night. All those things have been here before, some have been around forever; in any previous life, they would have been there.

We all have the same brains, and as far as we can tell, they work in the same sort of way in everyone. Hardly surprising then, that there are crowds of people out there who know they've lived before. It's a harmless kind of madness, unlikely to bother anyone, unless a person is convinced they were Ramses, or Genghis Kahn, and want to get the old regime back together.

Of course we have all been here before, some of us, part of us anyway. What goes around comes around. Every molecule in our bodies has had a former life, lots of them in fact, and not necessarily in people. It seems pretty unlikely that quantum energy has some embedded memory that knows what it did before. I'm pretty sure that religious notions of reincarnation don't come from quantum mechanics, but you never know. One of these days someone will figure it all out.

With a bit of luck some of me will be there.

It Comes

It comes. It's a simple enough line; you'd think anyone could get it right. Five hundred film extras, being paid, fed, clothed, and generally mollycoddled, certainly ought to be able to manage one line together.

You would think so, but somehow they never got it right. I don't know who had the bright idea that we should do the sound first. Five hundred people on a sound stage trying to say "It comes, it comes, it comes".

We spent hours trying to get them all in unison and actually sounding as though something was coming.

How hard can it be? Bloody hard, too bloody hard. We wasted a whole day and still we hadn't got a sound track. Thank heavens we did it on a Friday, at least we had a chance to work on it in the sound lab over the weekend before the same assembled multitude were supposed to be an unruly mob at the gates of the city chanting their simple line.

By Saturday evening it was starting to sound good, deep throated, hoarse and frightening. I relaxed and left the sound men to polish a little more.

Another mistake, as it turned out. They got carried away, that's the only word for it, or possibly they were taken over by some demon spirit. Personally, I doubt that, I mean, it was a Sunday, surely demon spirits take Sunday off?

By midmorning on Monday we had the assembled five hundred, suitable dressed in medieval rags and rather expensively applied imitation grime, milling about outside the city walls.

I should digress for a moment and point out that the city walls, although they are 12 feet high and look very ancient and terrifying, are in fact made of blocks of polystyrene, with a liberal application of a mixture of granite dust and wallpaper paste.

OK so we were all set to go, the multitude were about to start shouting, only this time we won't be recording them, but the sound boys decided to play the new sound track, just to get everyone in the mood.

I shouted, 'Roll 'em,' in the best Hollywood tradition and the sound erupted. I should never have let the nerds loose with all that kit. The most visceral, spine chilling voice screamed, 'It Comes, It comes,' over and over, but not just one voice, the whiz kids had multi tracked it, multi, multi, multi tracked it and added a screaming hoard of high-pitched females, for added emphasis.

Without going into too much detail about the script and the plot, which was never that hot to begin with, let's just say that the mob were supposed to be frightened. They were not supposed to panic and stampede, flattening twelve-foot walls, trampling the cameras into the mess and wrecking the rest of the set that we needed the next week.

Time for Plan B.

We hooked together the feed from four different cameras, right up until the medieval sandals kicked hell out of them. It made a great trailer. We re-wrote the plot, changed the title to "It Came" and made it a kind of time team, ancient horror, whodunit, with a bunch of bearded archaeologists trying to figure out what made the mess.

If they only knew.

Jobcentre Drag

One day at the Jobcentre is just like any other, boring, frustrating, and lacking in entertainment, until now anyway.

I was filling in another wretched form when the music started and seconds later I heard some one say, 'Please sit down, madam.'

The poor bureaucrat's voice could barely be heard above the din. The woman in the centre of the room had brought her own sound system, which was belting out a karaoke track for "Thank you for the music". Unless he could muster some amplification, the poor civil servant was unlikely to get much attention.

He retreated. Two minutes later he was back with a couple of security men and, somewhat amazingly, a megaphone. By now the woman had moved on to her second number, "Lily the Pink", which also involved waving a glass of wine around for the chorus. The assembled job seekers, always glad of some free entertainment, were joining in at full volume.

'Stop this noise,' from the megaphone, was greeted with loud boos.

The head of security wisely waited until the song was over before making his next move, and then lunged at the amplifier and just managed to hit the off switch.

'What the hell do you think you are doing?'

'That bloke on desk number three wanted to know what qualifications I had,' said the woman singer, sweeping off the wig and dropping her voice by an octave.

'What else could I do?'

It Must Be Lonely

I guess she must have had blond hair, they always do, at least in the movies, but that's not what I remember. From where I'm sitting, every step is a revelation. Have you ever pulled a magnet through iron filings? You know how every single piece of metal is dragged along and left in a new place, leaving a track that tells you exactly what happened.

I watched every eye in the place drawn around as she passed. Not staring, nothing crazy, they're not out on stalks as if this was a cartoon we were watching, just turned, coaxed, nudged, some overt stares but mostly surreptitious peeks from behind menus and newspapers and all in the same direction.

Some of the glances only lasted only a fraction of a second; others hung on longer, but each step hooked up a few more eyes. Step is the wrong word too. Some people walk from their knees down and the rest of their body rolls along like a sack on a trolley. Others swing their hips and stride. The whole of this woman walked. In the words of the song, she was poetry in motion. Her 'lovely locomotion', I'm still in the song here, started somewhere up near her chin and flowed from there.

A restaurant is a great place to be if you have that kind of walk. Navigating around tables and chairs gives just the right cues for hips to swing, shoulders and torso to twist and weave, and every part of her elegant presence to just look perfectly coordinated.

I remember the first time John Kennedy came to Europe with his wife. He made a joke. I think he said that he set off from America as the President and by the time he got to Paris he was that man with Jackie Kennedy. That was the kind of magnetism I was looking at.

All she wanted was a word with the waiter, ten tables away. She didn't have to tap him on the shoulder or anything like that. Long before she got to him—I guess if I'm being precise, that would be while she's passing table seven or eight—every eye on table ten is looking past the waiter at her. He turns like he is a robot, some sort of puppet on a stick, shoved around by all those eye lines streaking past his left shoulder. He's got no choice in the matter.

No one knows what she said to him. Maybe she wanted a glass of water, maybe the soup was cold. It only took a second to whisper something in his ear, and then she's turning away and the whole room is caught out. Now she'll see all the eyes on her back and it's rude to stare.

It's like she dropped a rock in a pond, actually like she's dropped a dozen rocks. One rock makes one set of ripples that spin out from the rock, so you always know where it was. A bunch of rocks make chaos with every ripple going different ways. Every eye in the place went about its own business, all looking for something to focus on, all trying not to look at her, because now she could be looking at them.

She walks back in a vacuum, every movement carving a new space in the attention of the room. At every table behind her she leaves eddies in the sounds of talk, like the wake of a boat leaving swirling water behind it. Defensive embarrassed looks and glances, wry smiles and hesitant coughs as different people realise they've lost the thread of their conversation.

Beauty is timeless, because time stands still when it goes by. Ageless because all the little slings and arrows that wear away the lives of normal people are stopped and spun and deflected. What destroys beauty in the end is what comes from inside and when we look at a woman like that, the inside is the one thing we have no chance of seeing.

It must be lonely.

On Women Bishops

Memo to Chief Executive.
Topic:- Horizon scanning and new risks.

As you may know, women bishops have been appointed in a number of countries where churches of the Anglican communion exist, Canada, Australia and New Zealand, for example, but also more unusual places such as Cuba and Swaziland. It can only be a matter of time before women bishops are appointed in England.

The inauguration of women bishops presents a number of complex and sensitive problems for our business. Fortunately, at the recent synod, through a combination of methods that we cannot disclose, we were able to secure a wafer-thin vote to prevent implementation in England this year and hence buy some time, but we must use this window while it is available.

The biggest difficulty for us is the style of dress. Bishops traditionally wear long robes that reach to the ground. Male and female bishops are therefore indistinguishable. This might lead one to suspect that our existing designs will suffice, but there is a significant risk that making no change will leave us vulnerable to a charge that we are failing to keep up with the times.

Bishop's headgear presents a similar problem. The mitre is traditional and we have no evidence that a new female version will appear.

We need to find ways to make it clear to our customers that we have accommodated our philosophy and designs to the new order.

I suggest that we commission a new design in which the female bishop has a waist to some degree. Obviously in real life, female bishops may not have a visible waist, because the ornamental vestments will obscure this, but a mere hint of a waist should suffice for our purpose. There is a risk that we will create rumours that female bishops are obliged to wear corsets, but the risk is small, and may well do no more than contribute to a few additional sales.

In the early years, women bishops will be a minority, so there is a dilemma as to whether we should market a small number, equivalent to the real world, or equal numbers of male and female models. For the sake of simplicity and avoidance of confusion, I propose that we manufacture equal numbers. This will simplify box design and make us appear forward looking by embracing equality.

I trust you will find this proposal acceptable.

Yours,

Rowan Welby, Chief Designer,

Chess Pieces International.

Send Someone Round With a Knife

I spent an interesting few minutes this morning being quizzed by some cold caller about my arthritis. I suspect he got my name via a book my wife ordered. Normally I would just hang up but I wanted to find out what he knew about arthritis and what he was selling.

Precious little was the answer to the first, and he was selling some sort of electronic device that would boost my circulation. Do I need that for damage to my wrist and fingers?

I found myself writing scripts for the conversation in my head.

'How does your arthritis affect you?' (His actual question.)

'Well I find firing a revolver is really painful these days, can't seem to aim straight, I may have to change over to a sawn-off shot gun but that seems so lacking in finesse.'

'Do you have any other disabilities?' (Again his actual question.)

'I get tinnitus as well, so what with not hearing the clicks and stiff fingers these days safe cracking is completely out.'

'Is it bad at any particular time of day?'

'Well I find I have no grip in the evening, which is the best time for cutting up and burying the bodies. I understand you can get knives with special grips for the disabled. Could you send someone round with one of those knives?'

I didn't try it, he'd probably call the cops, and I don't imagine they'd see the joke.

In the end, I just told him that it sounded as though his device was just another name for snake oil in a box, with flashing lights on it, and told him I wasn't interested.

It's so much easier to be horrible when one's writing fiction.

The Box in the Attic

I did wonder if it was cursed, or had a spell on it. I found a box in the attic full of jewels. They were old dark stones set in tarnished silver, strange trinkets hung on ancient links, and all tangled up in there so we had no idea if it was a necklace or a bracelet or just broken pieces. I had been clearing old insulation out of the loft; it was old fibreglass with what seemed like twenty years of dust on top of it and another hundred years worth underneath.

There weren't any diamonds, nothing flashed in the light as we took the lid off, just dull glows and sparkles from amber and jade and who knows what among the tangled chains. While I was looking at it I started to feel unwell, and in another ten minutes I had a fever and shaking. One moment I'm sitting in an armchair in the house, happy at a good day's work all done and waiting to eat the supper I can smell. The next moment I'm shivering, overcome by rigors, teeth chattering, clutching every part of me together to try to stay warm, feeling chilled to the bone on a midsummer's day.

How the box came to be there took time to discover; the house is old so it might have been there a hundred years or more. Perhaps it never should have been disturbed but there's no going back now.

It was leaning on a wall upstairs started it. It's an innocent enough thing, leaning on a wall, until the wall moves. Don't let me exaggerate, it didn't set off for the next county, it just moved an inch, and if you leaned harder it moved another inch and came back when you stood up straight. No way a wall like that can stay in a bedroom, so it had to go. After than it was obvious that the ceiling had problems. It sagged. It hung like a blanket, like the roof of a desert sheik's tent, three inches lower in the middle than it was at the sides. That moved too, not that we tried very hard. Standing under a ceiling and pushing it up and down a couple of inches is hard hat work, and not for the fainthearted. We climbed up in the loft to examine the problem from above. Dirty old fibreglass insulation covered the floor, but pull that aside and under a century's dust you could see where the ceiling had come away from the rafters. All that held it up were the ancient laths embedded in the plaster, that and the woodworms holding hands.

Of course it was worse than that, the rafters were coming away from the joists as well. It all had to go, and that's how we found the box.

It's not really fair to call it a treasure chest. That gives the wrong idea about size. This wasn't some massive structure, weighed down with iron bands around venerable oak planks. Such a thing would have fallen through the decrepit canopy long ago. It was smaller than that, two hands could get around it and barely cover the wood and metal bands, but it looked the part. As we tore the ceiling down and ripped away the old insulation, it came down with the dead spiders and the dust. We almost missed it. I wore a facemask and a respirator and a Tyvek suit. As the demolition went on, the room filled with dust. It got so dark I could hardly see from one end to the other and the floor disappeared under a carpet of broken laths, torn insulation, archaic horsehair plaster and dust. So much dust—choking, black and pervasive dust.

Sitting in the heap was the box. Without the metal bands we might have missed it, but the dust slid off the metal and even in the fog it gleamed enough, as though it knew the time had come to be found.

The fever and shaking chills went on for almost an hour. Using every coat and blanket we could find in the house made little difference. Lois took a picture of me huddled in the armchair, shaking and shivering. I looked like an elderly Inuit swathed in multiple coverings, hooded over as though I were in the Arctic and not summer in Worcestershire. I watched her worry. I drank sweet tea and I shook from head to toe. Another ten minutes and she would have called an ambulance but it finally passed and left me weary to the bone.

It must have been some sort of allergy to the dust. Easy to say in hindsight, but in the thick of it a spell or a curse was just as convincing. How did the box get there? Like everything else in this house one thing leads to another.

The previous owner had read somewhere that when you go on holiday the best way to hide your valuables is to put them in a box and stuff them under the insulation in the loft. Burglars are unlikely to look there.

It's easy to do and you just have to remember where you put them. If you are starting to get Alzheimer's disease, the remembering is the hard part. It was the Alzheimer's that made them sell the house and hence we bought it. It was the Alzheimer's that stopped him maintaining and repairing the house, hence the sagging ceilings and worn out fabric.

We took the box back to the former owners and they told us the story. The curious antique jewels were family mementos, trinkets bought to celebrate children's births and other valued events. Such things have a life of their own and a meaning that comes from memory. The box wasn't cursed, it was charmed and it needed to find its way home.

The Nun, the Glass of Wine and the Fête

'Have you heard the one about the nun and the glass of wine at the village fête?'

'Is that the one where the drunk mistakes the nun for a penguin?'

I shake my head, buy the guy another drink and move on. They do good beer here; brew it themselves out back, so I have another one myself. No sense in rushing.

This kind of detective work is 90% shoe leather and 10% inspiration, that and a lot of driving. It's not all pubs of course; some of the material comes from keeping your ear to the ground in unlikely places. It requires great patience too. Sometimes I'm on the road for a week.

You need eyes in the back of your head, that's the other thing, you never know when the competition are on to something and they're damn good at disguising themselves. I've been fooled a few times, I'll admit it, but usually I notice the little things and I can get in some sort of spoiler, something to ruin their day. You've got to take your little pleasures where you can.

Of course, that would never work if they spotted who I was, so I'm pretty hot with the subterfuge myself. I've tried those latex masks, the kind that make you look like someone completely different, but they're hard work and take a long time to apply. Most of the time, I make do with glasses, hairstyle and accents. The trouble is that can mess up the primary task. It's important to fit in, get people's confidence, so it doesn't pay to come up with a look that's too weird. It's a sophisticated business.

The other thing you need is a hell of a memory. There is no way you can be taking notes when you're close to the good stuff. It has to be in your head. Of course I write it all up before I go to bed, even if I've had to imbibe a few in the course of duty. That's not as easy as it sounds because I use code to make sure it's safe. You never know when some of the opposition might try and make a grab for it.

It has to be quite a complicated code, a bit like writing music; you have to have some way of getting down the subtle details. These days the technology is really helping; I can carry a tape recorder so small that you'd never know it was there. One of these days someone's going to figure out how to wire me up so I don't have to do a thing except be in the right place and close enough to the action to pick up every subtle sound.

There you have it, everything you need to know about the joke collecting business. I'm still looking for the one about the nun, the glass of wine and the fête; have you heard it?

The World's Worst Hit Man

'Grandpa, who was the world's worst hit man?'

'Son, what do you mean by worst? Do you mean the scariest, nastiest, worst criminal of them all or someone who couldn't hit a barn door at the end of his arm?'

The old man laughed, a slow throaty chuckle followed by a deep smile. 'Well I guess whatever way you see it, Jimmy the Magician Murphy, or Magic Murphy as he was sometimes known, he'd be my favourite. Magic Murphy made more people disappear than you can count, but no one knows how he did it.

'It's a mystery, even to this day. Mystery could have been his middle name, except Magic stuck to him sooner. No one knew what he looked like. They had his voice right enough, the FBI had tapes of bad guys making contracts with him, so they knew his voice. It was kind of wheezy, and maybe a Brooklyn accent underneath. Couldn't mistake him, but that's all they ever got.

'No one ever found a body, no blood, no cartridge cases, no fingerprints, no nothing. These days they'd have been looking for DNA but my guess is they wouldn't have found a trace. That was the magic, he didn't just make people disappear, he made everything go.

'There was another thing about him, he'd turn some jobs down, if it was just one mobster chasing another, well Jimmy would pass on it. I guess he didn't want to make enemies in the wrong places. You look at the history of all the famous hit men and they all get hit themselves. Jimmy had more sense, wouldn't play that game.

'Now if a mob boss wanted to get rid of one of his own men, say if he thought the guy had been ratting to the Feds, why then Magic was your man, he'd make them disappear in no time. One day the guy would be around, and the next day he'd be gone without a trace. If he had a family they'd be gone too. Wiped off the face of the earth, and no one ever found any of them.

'Most folk thought he must have a big vat of acid somewhere, so he could dissolve the bodies, flush them away.

'They looked; the mob looked, the cops looked, all of them looked real hard, but they never found a thing. It had to be an old factory they thought, or something like. Maybe a warehouse by a river, who knows, they never found it.

'Some folks thought he might have a truck, you know, like a petrol tanker, only full of acid. He could roll up, park it nearby, grab the mark, who ever it was, chuck them in the tank and drive around as long as he liked. The body would be in the back there, sloshing around, the acid getting stirred every time he went round a curve or stopped in the traffic, everything dissolving away to nothing. Some time later he could flush them away somewhere and they're never seen again.

'I reckon he'd have all the papers and those signs on the back that tell you about dangerous cargo, so no one in their right mind is gonna want to peep in or drain it out.

'You know those big tankers have beds in the back of the cab, so he could sleep anywhere, move around the country, park some place to pull a job, and be away on the road before you know it.'

'How do you know that, Grandpa?'

'I'm making it up, son, but if anyone ever asks you about Magic Murphy that's the story to tell. They'll believe you, they always believed me.'

'OK, Grandpa, that's what I'll say. Now what's the real story?'

'Simple, kid, I think he worked for the Feds; he made people disappear into witness protection programmes, took the money off the mob for each hit, and collected the evidence against them at the same time.'

'How do you know all this, Grandpa?'

'Never you mind. Now do you wanna camp out in the old tanker truck tonight?'

There's a Hole in my Phone

My mum's phone has an intermittent fault. It sometimes cuts out in mid conversation and sometimes it doesn't ring.

I have tried to report this.

I rang BT. They ask me what number I am calling about, then take me though umpteen menus ending up by telling me that it is not a BT line, so they can't help.

After four attempts, trying different menus and coming at it via the 100-operator number or through the 0800 route, I always end up being shut out in the same way. So far, all I have talked to are tape recorders.

So, I phoned Tesco, who do my calls, after a couple of false starts when their tape recorder told me they were closed, but open every day at times that included my call, a conversation with a friendly human actually took place. They couldn't help either unless I knew who was the provider for my mum's calls.

Why don't I phone her up and ask her? Because her phone isn't working. I am reminded of that song, 'There's a Hole in my Bucket.'

My next attempt was to call Ofcom.

BT or Tesco can't pass on my fault report to my mum's provider because it would infringe competition rules. One provider can't know who is providing to other numbers, so a fragmented system that does not connect is official policy.

All they need is a central fault service that is independent of the phone providers. I suspect that a computer and a few tape recorders could do it.

How did we manage to set up a telephone service where competition is more important than service?

The insurance companies have a central fund to deal with car crashes involving uninsured drivers, and all those companies are in competition—ask any meerkat.

So why can't the phone operators have a way of dealing with faults that is fool proof?

I at least have done my bit and suggested to Ofcom that they might look into it. It is their responsibility to regulate the whole system. My guess is that I won't hear anything from them and nothing will be done. I suspect that the underlying assumption is that we all have mobile phones and can fend for ourselves.

The Ofcom chap implied that I should know who was providing my mum's calls, so I asked him if he knew the provider of his mum and anyone else he cared about. No answer to that.

'Can't you phone her?'

'There's a hole in my bucket, dear Lisa, dear Lisa.'

There's a Lion Outside

I had an old motorcycle; a side valve ex-army BSA that I suspect had actually been in the war. It was a 500cc single-cylinder machine, with girder front forks that scared the hell out of you when they went over a big bump. Girder forks look like something stolen off the Manhattan Bridge, all struts and springs and everything moves as you go along. In the winter of 1963, after hammering over rutted snow for four months, enough threads were stripped from important places that the whole thing fell to bits, luckily at ten miles an hour. I spun round 180 degrees in the road, managed to avoid falling off and eventually had the old thing hauled off to the scrap yard.

I mention this to convey the sort of anxiety involved in driving this ancient machine. In the summer of '61 I took it camping. Complete with a sidecar packed up with tent, sleeping bag, luggage and girlfriend. We could do about forty-three miles an hour on the straight bits. I went with other friends who had solo bikes.

My ancient machine had to carry all the kit, so Porlock Hill included smoke coming out of the clutch and even more angst than usual. It took all day to get to Cornwall and by the time we camped I was exhausted. Not only were my friends new to motorcycles, they'd never erected a tent either and I soon found they were slow learners, slow at everything except larking about, getting drunk and having no idea how to cook.

Things got worse through the night, what with airbeds that deflated, and alcohol induced loquacity. Crammed into one tent we all got on each other's nerves through a restless night and were woken early by the summer dawn. Those who tried to stay asleep were forced awake by those who had to find some essential item in bags that were always in the wrong place. By six am I think everyone was ready to go home; we desperately needed some unifying event, something to restore camaraderie and goodwill. It came from a most unlikely source.

Mel decided he had to pee, struggled over the other protesting bodies and unzipped the tent.

Buried in our sleeping bags the rest of us turned over and rejoiced in the extra room for a few seconds, but were jolted awake by a gasp. The sort of sound someone makes when they've been bitten by a snake or almost shot.

'There's a lion at the door.'

Dragging ourselves round to look, we could see a patch of sunshine framed by two furry legs, with two more a long way further back.

The silence was broken by a kind of panting licking sound.

Actually it was a St Bernard, nearly as big as a lion, but rather more friendly and enough to make us all laugh for the rest of the week.

What Did They Expect?

My grandfather dug coal deep under a Welsh valley. Back then coal was cut by hand, sometimes in seams only a few feet high, the miners working in the dark almost lying down to get at the coal.

Above the mine the hills and valleys stretch away, sweeping views over craggy rocks and narrow green pastures. Sheep do well there. Another part of my family made cloth, woollen cloth that they sold way down the valley where the big towns cluster along the coast.

My grandmother's father used to take the pony and trap with bundles of cloth to sell. When he died, my great grandmother took over. My first name is her surname, because my dad promised her.

The first time she came home from the market she had difficulty with the horse. A short way along the road he stopped. The nearest building was a pub, so Great Grandma went inside to see if anyone knew what to do. When she came out the horse was happy to move on. He stopped again at the next pub, and the one after. It didn't take her long to work out the answer, so at each pub, she stopped, went in, came out and they moved on. My grandfather later in life was teetotal. It makes sense when you know the story.

Knowing the story made sense of the killings too.

The first death was a sheep, found at the bottom of a ravine, smashed, torn apart and with huge chunks of flesh missing. No one paid it any mind. Sheep are daft creatures and some are bound to fall down cliffs occasionally. I only discovered the record by accident; the local vet had had been called when the dead animal was first seen; he rapidly concluded that nothing could be done, but he made a note that I found years later.

There were four similar deaths before the one that caused some notoriety. That time four sheep were killed and it made it into the newspapers.

It was really a random chance that put me onto the story. I'd been to a conference in Pembrokeshire and crossing the heads of the valleys road on the way home a sudden whim took me down the old road, past the pit where Grandpa worked. I stopped in the little village, parked the car and strolled around. It was a sorry sight in many ways. The place was deserted, most of the population had moved away when the pit was closed. I picked up a newspaper and stopped for a cup of tea in a little cafe. The paper was as boring as the town, but one article caught my eye. You know how it is with local papers, sometimes there isn't enough news and they have to stuff it with fillers, like a whole page on 'Fifty years ago on this day.'

Most of the page was full of a horrific murder; a body at the bottom of a ravine, smashed and torn about, with parts missing. Sensational stuff, but of course because it was a human body it had to be recovered, identified, autopsied and properly buried. After some detective work it turned out to be a tourist and it was assumed that he must have strayed off the track and fallen into the ravine. After hearing some gory evidence and quizzing the local police and the vet, the coroner concluded that a wild animal must have dragged off the missing body parts. There was some speculation, maybe a wild dog or a wild cat perhaps. The vet stated that he had seen similar wounds on dead sheep and somehow that made it acceptable. No further searching was done. It was recorded as accidental death. In a statement afterwards the local bobby gave a cautionary tale about the need for local knowledge and the folly of walking on the hills unaccompanied.

'This is not the first case,' he said. 'I don't know how we can get the message across, but walking on these hills in the late evening or at night is hazardous. Even though it was a full moon, there was not enough light to be sure of your footing. Some of the ground can give way easily, and we do get subsidence because of the mining.'

It set me thinking and I took the paper home. That was fifty years ago and there had been cases before. Were there more after that?

I don't know why I became so fascinated, maybe it was the family connection, maybe it was just that the story had loose ends, but I found myself drawn into it.

I could go on for days, rambling through the turns and twists that I uncovered but you'd only get bored, or frightened.

I found more than a dozen cases, spread over more then fifty years and all of them were almost identical. A body at the bottom of a ravine or the foot of a crag, smashed, torn to pieces and with parts missing. Always a stranger, never a local. There were more sheep too, and they fitted the same pattern.

No obvious connection had ever been found; occasionally the previous cases were referred to, but there was never any sign of foul play, in the traditional sense. No sign of knife wounds or bullet holes, no evidence of strangling or blunt trauma from a weapon. Always the damage from the fall and the body too mangled to say what exactly had caused the death. In every case they had died before they hit the bottom of the cliff. There were no pools of blood, no signs of struggle or movement. They all hit the ground after their heart had stopped.

I read back through local history and found a strange thing. All the cases happened when the mine was closed. Sometimes it was a strike, sometimes it was a public holiday, or an accident underground or a breakdown, but all the deaths happened when the mine was closed, and they all happened within a day or two of a full moon.

What made me think of that you ask? The evidence was there in the inquests, it was mentioned several times and I checked the rest. They put it down to fools from far away imagining that the moon gave enough light to see.

Ten years ago there were four cases in successive months and then they stopped altogether. Ten years ago the mine closed.

It took me a month to get up the nerve to go back and I made sure I picked a date halfway between the full moons.

Before I made the trip I checked out the parish records and identified the oldest residents, people that I knew had been there all their lives. Some of them might even have known my grandfather.

I found one talkative old codger in the only pub that was still open and loosened his tongue still further with alcohol. Eventually, when I thought the moment was right, and when I was sure he was too drunk to be dangerous, I took a risk and asked. 'Ten years ago, when those four tourists died, it was werewolves wasn't it.'

For a long moment he looked at me.

'They were all English,' he said, 'what did they expect.'

'What did they expect?'

'Closing the pit like that, the bastard English, took all our coal and closed the pit.'

I had no idea where this was going, so tried the old trick of letting silence ask the questions.

'They were great lads,' he said, 'bloody strong, worked the night shift for years, down to the pit before dark, twelve hours work and out again at sun up. Never took holidays, worked all the time. Never saw the moon; and then the English bastards closed the pit. What did they expect.'

'The pit had been closed before.'

He nodded, lost in his thoughts or the beer for a minute.

'The boys did their best,' he said. 'Took sheep most of the time, and never a local. Never a local.'

I waited, hoping for more but he was staring at the bottom of his glass.

I bought another round.

'What happened to them?'

He looked at me and grinned.

'Worried are you?'

'I'm local really, my grandfather worked in that mine, my dad was born here.'

'I might have guessed. Who else would come here. You're safe enough anyway,' he said. 'They moved to France, got jobs working in the wine business. They have bloody great caves you know, go on for miles underground, and they always need strong blokes who can work all night.'

What Shall It Profit?

'What shall it profit a man if he gains the whole world and loses his soul?'

'You askin' me that? Daft question. Bloke must be in the wrong business. I mean I've heard of getting through shoe leather, but losing the whole sole, that's extreme, man. Shoes are a legit expense. You can chalk it up to the taxman long before the sole's worn through.

'That really is wrong the business though, there's no money to be made in door-to-door sales. Get on a computer—trade paper—whizz electrons around. I can sell you a chit for a thousand pairs of shoes and it fits in your pocket, couple of strokes on a keyboard and Bob's your uncle.'

'I don't think they meant that kind of sole.'

'What's the other kind?'

'Your soul, your deeper feelings, your sense of self.'

'You mean like in soul music. Yeah you've got a point there. I mean I remember weeks when I was trading hard, all that caffeine and I was still so tired I couldn't tell you what music was on the radio. Never knew what to play in the car. All sounded the same. Could have played a cash register for all I knew. Yeah you could lose your soul that way.

'But hell, take a client to a concert, chalk that up to expenses too. Take 'em to a whole bloody pop festival, no sweat. Mind you, none of that mud and tents stuff, fly in with a chopper or cruise down in a limmo, all goes on the slate, probably set up a meet with some of the singers. Soul, rock, classical, I got all the contacts, have your soul back in no time, man.'

'He means your soul, your inner self, the thing that sets you apart from the animals.'

'I tell you what sets me apart from the animals, mate, making money, that's what. Mind you some of those traders are animals, when they say dog eat dog they are serious man.'

'But what about your inner self.'

'Where the hell is this going? Who said this stuff anyway?'

'Saint Mark.'

'You mean some geezer in Palestine couple of thousand years ago, that St Mark?'

'That's the one, have you read him?'

'Nah. But he's a clever bugger ain't he. Think about it, what a line. You got to hand it to those boys, always on the make; bloody good at it too, the church back then took ten per cent of everything, any objection and they'll set God on you and now you tell me they're after my soul. Cool stuff, what a way to spook the opposition.'

'What?'

'A quote like that'd have you looking over your shoulder all the time, wouldn't it. It might be just enough to put you off going for the kill in a deal. Smart, anything to get an edge. You got to admire it. I'll tell you what through. If I lose my soul, I'll hire a few private detectives to get out there and find it. I'll bloody chalk that up to expenses too.'

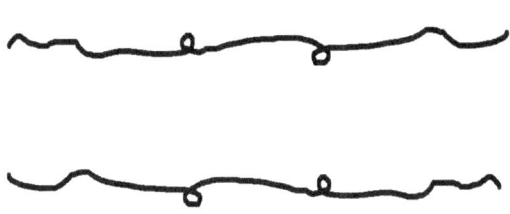

www.ingramcontent.com/pod-product-compliance
Lightning Source LLC
Chambersburg PA
CBHW070345130626
46556CB00007B/3035